On a Hot Summer Day

Joe, age fourteen:

Me and a few friends were out in the middle of the river when we saw some guys on the shore, hollering at us.

"Help," they said. "Someone's drowning, and we can't swim!"

I moved closer to shore, treading water—the water was really muddy, you couldn't see a thing. . . .

In a second, I felt my feet run across the top of his head. I dove and saw he was stuck in the mud at the very bottom of the river. The guy was big—he was eighteen or nineteen years old—and he was heavy. Finally I pulled him out and up to the surface of the water.

After we got him to shore I asked if anybody knew CPR. Martin's thirteen, and he learned CPR in the Boy Scouts. So I told Martin to give the guy CPR and pretty soon we got the water out of his lungs and stomach.

I sent one of the guys to go get a rescue squad. By the time they came, this guy was sitting up and breathing on his own.

Other Books by Neal Shusterman

Dissidents
It's O.K. to Say No to Cigarettes and Alcohol
Neon Angel—The Cherie Currie Story
  (with Cherie Currie)
The Shadow Club
Speeding Bullet
What Daddy Did

KID HEROES

True
Stories
of
Rescuers,
Survivors,
and
Achievers

NEAL SHUSTERMAN

TOR

A TOM DOHERTY ASSOCIATES BOOK
NEW YORK

KID HEROES

Copyright © 1991 by RGA Publishing Group, Inc.

A Tor Book
Published by Tom Doherty Associates, Inc.
175 Fifth Avenue
New York, N.Y. 10010

Tor ® is a registered trademark of Tom Doherty Associates, Inc.

ISBN: 0-812-50994-3
Library of Congress Catalog Card Number: 90-48780

First edition: March 1991
First mass market printing: August 1993

Printed in the United States of America

0 9 8 7 6 5 4 3 2 1

Contents

Acknowledgments   vii
Introduction   ix
Rescuers   1
Survivors   59
Achievers   89
Tomorrow's Hero   171
Bibliography   174

Acknowledgments

I would like to thank the following heroes:

First of all, I would like to thank Janet Simowitz, Daniel Jones, Brian Flemming, Michael Varnen, and Elaine Shusterman—the *Kid Heroes* staff. Without their invaluable research and hard work, this book would have been very, very thin.

I would also like to thank Kristina Linden and Beth Rasgorshek, editors of *Young American: America's Newspaper for Kids*; Lela Katzman and Hasbro's G.I. Joe Search for Real American Heroes; Ken Melius of Melius & Peterson Publishing; Walter F. Rutkowski and the Carnegie Hero Fund Commission; Ruby Blair at Optimist International; Colette Pederson at Celebrities Against Cancer; Hal Wingo at *People* magazine; Lari Johnson and the Invent America Awards; and coach Bill Greene. All these people, organizations, and publications provided friendly assistance and needed material.

I'd like to thank the Aliengena family for their

hospitality, as well as Kelly Lyons, the Alexander family, David and Sam "Ricky Rocko" Rogoway, and all those kids whose interviews fill this book. Thanks, all of you, for taking the time to speak with me. I found each of your interviews, as well as this entire project, ennobling and inspirational!

Introduction:
Normal People

On one dark October night, a car flips off a bridge and lands upside down, its roof smashed. Somehow a five-year-old boy finds the courage and strength to practically drag his injured mother out of the car and up a steep muddy slope to save her live.

A girl tragically loses both legs below the knee as a baby, yet at the age of fourteen is the youngest member of the United States Olympic Team.

A nine-year-old boy decides he wants to become the world's youngest pilot—then decides he wants to be the youngest person to fly across the country and back—and then sets out to be the first private pilot ever to fly across the entire Soviet Union.

None of these kids are superheroes. None of these kids were born with powers and abilities far beyond those of mortal kids. They're just run-of-the-mill, everyday, normal people. They go to school, they watch TV, they play video games, and they worry about zits, grades, braces, and their allowance just like anyone else.

In fact, one of these "kid heroes" could be you.

"What?" I hear you cry. "Me, a hero? *Me?* I'm the substitute player on the league's worst baseball team! Me, a hero? I'm the shortest girl in school! Me? I got all 'Z's' on my report card! Me? I've never even *tried* Wheaties, The Breakfast of Champions! Me, a hero? Ha!"

The truth is, you never really know what you can do—until you do it. Quiet people have come through in emergency situations, while loud, take-charge people have stood around not knowing what to do. Kids whom no one considered exceptionally talented or intelligent have accomplished the most amazing things.

The dictionary defines *hero* as a person whose courage, strength, or achievement is outstanding—courage enough to perform a rescue, strength enough to overcome and survive adversity, or the achievement of *someone* determined to make a mark on the world.

This book is divided into those three sections: rescuers, survivors, and achievers. All of the kids in this book are real. Each of them will show you what amazing things an everyday, normal kid can do.

RESCUERS

The first part of this book is dedicated to kids who were in the right place at the right time, with the right amount of courage, and the right amount of luck.

They thought quickly, moved quickly, and saved someone's life.

The first story is about a young girl who survived an awful ordeal and miraculously rescued her older sister from the crushed cabin of an airplane. . . .

The Ordeal of Tammy Crites

The Cessna 172 airplane takes off from Banff National Park, in Canada, in high winds. It heads south, toward Montana . . . but the plane is not going to make it.

From the very beginning, Dr. Crites, his two daughters, and his wife know that it is not going to be an easy flight. The plane is bouncing up and down violently, shook by the unpredictable winds. Six-year-old Tammy Crites and her eleven-year-old sister, Korrina, begin to worry. Their father reassures them, telling them that everything will be all right. Dr. Crites is an excellent pilot, but he isn't very experienced—he's only had his pilot's license for a few months.

Realizing that his small plane is unable to fight the fierce winds, Dr. Crites decides to fly low, cutting a smoother course beneath the winds . . .

. . . And before anyone knows what's happening, the plane is grazing the treetops. One wing smashes into the trunk of a tall tree, and Dr. Crites loses control of the plane, ending the flight just minutes after it began.

In an instant, Tammy Crites's world is torn apart and turned upside down.

The small plane goes down in rough, steep terrain, crashing onto its battered roof in the middle of a creek. No one sees the accident. No one knows the plane has gone down. The family is miles from anyone who can help them.

Tammy, still strapped into her seat, hanging upside down from her seat belt, tries to get her parents' attention. She pulls her mother's hair, but there is no response. In a moment she knows that neither of her parents survived the crash. Only she and her sister are alive.

Tammy frees herself from her seat belt and hurries to Korrina. Korrina is badly injured: her wrist, cheekbone, and jaw are broken. Her skull is fractured. There is no way for Tammy to help her parents now, but maybe she can help Korrina. Tammy herself has a broken collarbone and bruises all over, but she will not let that stop her.

She struggles to move her father and then fights to free Korrina from the twisted wreckage.

The creek outside the shattered plane is cold. Korrina cannot wade to shore, so Tammy quickly comes up with a plan. She grabs what luggage she can find and uses the luggage to float her older sister to shore.

Once on shore, Korrina can go no farther, so Tammy sets out by herself, into the woods, searching for help. Korrina has started to shiver, and Tammy knows that if she doesn't find help soon, Korrina will die.

Ignoring the pain from her injuries, Tammy makes her way through the canyon—a canyon with walls twenty feet high on either side. She is in the middle of nowhere, but she has to find help.

Tammy begins to call out at the top of her lungs, hoping someone will hear her. For more than an hour she calls, but it appears that there is no one nearby.

Far, far away, three women hiking through the woods hear Tammy's cries, but try as they might, they can't find Tammy. Realizing that something must be wrong, they immediately report the cries to the park warden.

Without a moment to lose, Scott Ward, the park's warden, sets out by helicopter to find the person in trouble. Finally he spots Tammy.

Ward drops into the canyon and rescues Tammy and Korrina.

If it hadn't been for Tammy, everyone is certain that Korrina would not have survived—she was suffering from "hypothermia," or loss of body heat, as well as her injuries.

Because no one knew that the plane had gone down, a search might not have been mounted for days. If it hadn't been for Tammy's quick thinking, this story would have turned out differently!

Newsflash!

POUGHKEEPSIE, NEW YORK—In the freezing air of this icy winter, five-year-old Sean Kingsley saved the life of his three-year-old cousin, Casey, when Casey fell into a deep dry well.

The two were having a snowball fight when Casey slipped through the snow and into the well. As she slid down, Sean ran to Casey and caught her hand. Although Sean weighed only forty-eight pounds and Casey weighed thirty-five, Sean was able to keep hold of Casey's hand as she dangled in the deep well. Casey was too heavy for Sean to pull out, so he just held on, while the two of them screamed for help.

It was five minutes before help arrived, before the kids' grandmother heard their distant cries. But at last Casey was rescued, unharmed.

Had Sean not tightly grasped her hand as she dangled helplessly over the black pit, Casey would have disappeared into the deep hole of that awful well.

The River and Joe Memory

It was a hot summer day, just like any other hot summer day for fourteen-year-old Joe Memory and his friends. The last thing anyone would expect on a hot, lazy summer day would be to become a hero. . . .

Me and a few friends of mine were out in the middle of the river playing in a canoe. We had turned it over, and were pulling it in to shore, when we saw some guys—about five of them—on the shore. They were hollering at us.

"Help," they said. "Someone's drowning, and we can't swim!"

At first I thought they were just playing, but they were real serious about it.

If someone was drowning, I figured the current might have pulled him out a little bit, so I swam around the middle of the river—you see, the guys on shore said they didn't know where he was at.

He wasn't out that far, so they told me to come in a little bit. I moved closer to shore and dove down, but I still couldn't find him. I moved closer, still treading water—the water was really muddy here, you couldn't see a thing—and then I saw little bubbles come up. . . . In a second, I felt my feet run across the top of his head! I went down again, and saw he was stuck two or three feet into the mud at the very bottom of the river. The guy was big—he was eighteen or nineteen years old—and he was heavy. I almost couldn't pull him up. I went down again, and finally I pulled him out—I snatched him out from the mud and pulled him up to the surface of the water. Then I called to someone to come and help me.

We got him to shore. The guy wasn't moving. He was unconscious, and we couldn't hear any heartbeat. He didn't have any pulse.

I asked somebody if they knew CPR [cardiopulmonary resuscitation], and Martin, who had been with me in the canoe, said he did. Martin's thirteen, and he learned CPR in the Boy Scouts. So I told Martin to give him CPR, and pretty soon we got the water out of his lungs and stomach. When we did that, he started throwing up—he started breathing though, a little bit at first, and then a little more.

After that, we sent one of the guys to go get a rescue squad. By the time they came, this guy was sitting up and breathing on his own. They took him home, but two hours later they carried him to the

Columbus County Hospital, where he stayed about a week with pneumonia.

Joe and his friend won the Governor's Medal of Honor for their rescue, as well as the Scouting Medal of Honor.

Newsflash!

UPPER DARBY, PENNSYLVANIA—A robbery was thwarted yesterday when Katrin Hubenthal, age thirteen, ran to the aid of sixty-three-year-old Lucille Hanger.

The incident occurred on a busy street during rush hour. Two women were robbing Miss Hanger at gunpoint, and although there were many witnesses, no one stopped to help. From across the street, Katrin saw the robbery and told her mother to call the police. Then Katrin ran to Lucille Hanger's aid. The robbers fled when they saw that Katrin had come to help Miss Hanger.

Before Katrin arrived, one of the assailants hit Lucille Hanger twice on the head with the gun. While she was not seriously hurt, she was extremely shaken by the attack.

Katrin thought the thieves got away with Miss Hanger's purse. However, later, when Katrin was talking to the police, she discovered that, thanks to her, the thieves were unable to get away with anything.

Katrin had seen the criminals well enough to give an accurate description to the police and, with the help of Katrin's description, the two assailants were identified and brought to justice.

Katrin received several awards, including two from the police department.

Rocky Lyons:
The Little Boy
Who Could

Football superstar Marty Lyons has always been a hero to kids, as both a football player and the founder of an organization that grants the last wishes of terminally ill children. Little did he know that his five-year-old son, Rocky, was about to become a hero as well.

Rocky loved the story The Little Engine That Could, *and one dark, scary night, Rocky used the lesson he learned from that story to save his mother's life.*

Rocky's mom tells of that night. . . .

It was the night before Halloween. Rocky and I had gone out to dinner with some friends. It was a little before eleven when we left, taking Highway 43 home. Highway 43 is a really dark road. It goes over a river, and near the river both sides of the road fall off into bar pits—deep ditches on either side. When it rains, there's usually residual water from the river in these huge ditches, but unfortunately we had been about fifty days without rain.

It was especially dark that night—there weren't any stars or anything. Suddenly the Ford pickup I was driving hit a pothole, and the right front wheel ran off the road. The wheel sank right into the ash at the side of the road—it was so soft it was like powder.

Rocky was asleep, laying down in his seat. His head was up against the passenger door, and his feet were in my lap. Neither of us were wearing our seat belts.

When the front tire ran off the road, I turned the wheel as far as I could, trying to get back onto the road, but Rocky's tennis shoe was caught in the steering wheel, wedging the wheel to the left. Well, when that happened, I knew we were going to flip immediately.

I had a feeling that it was going to be bad.

I laid down on top of Rocky on the floor as the truck flipped. We slid about twenty yards down the road on the driver's side of the truck. That's when we hit the edge of the bridge, and we began to flip over and over—I don't have any idea how many times it flipped; it just kept going over and over, I thought it would never stop.

When we stopped, the roof had been crushed, and was only eight inches above the seats. Had we not been lying down, we would have been dead immediately.

I think what kept Rocky safe was that he was

asleep. He really didn't fully awaken until the truck had completely stopped. He didn't have time to see what had happened and get scared—I mean, by the time he was awakened by the jolt, it was all over with.

When Rocky got up off the floorboard and scrambled out of the truck, he said, "Mama, look—the wheels are pointed up to the sky," but I had so much blood in my eyes I couldn't see—I really thought I was blind. All I could feel was heat in my eyes and pain everywhere else. I couldn't feel my face—one shoulder was practically ripped off, and the other one was crushed, so I couldn't raise my hands at all.

I told Rocky to jump away from the truck, and run as far away from it as he could, 'cause I didn't know if it was going to blow up.

I was bleeding to death, and all I kept thinking was that I just wanted to lie there in the truck and sleep for a while. If I did, I guess I would have never woken up.

Rocky got out of the truck, thought for a bit, and said, "I can see how to get you of here—if you'll just let me help you, I can see how to get you out." So he crawled back into the truck, got behind me and pushed me out the window. I couldn't see, but Rocky could. Like most things, Rocky took this all with a really level head.

Anyway, he looked around and said, "We've got to get you up the hill. We've got to get you to a hospital, Mama."

I was worried about him—I was worried that he was hurt—after all, I couldn't see him.

"Mama, I'm fine . . . I'm all right," he said.

So we tried getting up the hill, which was quite an ordeal because I did not have the use of either arm. I had no balance and no strength. I'd dig my fingers in the dirt, and try to pull myself up the hill, but I couldn't do it, because of my arms.

Then I turned to Rocky and said, "Rocky, don't let anything scare you, just tell me—look at Mom, and tell me if I've got two arms." You see, I couldn't feel my left hand.

"Yeah, you do," he says. He picked up my left arm and put it up against my face. I couldn't feel it at all.

Rocky knew I was in bad shape, so he got behind me and pushed me about a foot up the hill.

"I don't think I can make it," I told him. "There's no way I can make it up that hill."

"Okay," he said. "I'll go up the hill, and try to get a car."

So he took off running up this hill. Then I thought about how dark it was, and I thought, *He's only five, he's gonna get hit by a car out in the middle of the road!* I was praying for him to come back.

He couldn't stop a car, so he came back and began to push me up the hill again.

"Rocky," I said, "I don't think I can do it." And that's when he talked to me about the train.

When he was little, *The Little Engine That Could*

was always his favorite story. Every time he would come to me and say, "Mama, I can't do something," I would always say to him, "Rocky, think about that little train," so he was accustomed to hearing that. Well, now he brought that lesson back to me!

"Mama, think about the train," he said, "I think I can . . . I think I can . . . I think I can . . . I think I can."

And so I kept thinking that I could do it, until finally he got me up out of the ditch to the edge of the road—I had been lying on my stomach, and he just about pushed me up that hill, 'cause I couldn't use my arms at all.

Once we were up top, Rocky helped me to my feet, and we tried to flag down a car. The first car that passed did not stop, and neither did the second car . . . but the headlights lit me up well enough for Rocky to see me. That's the first time that he quivered. He looked at me and said, "Oh my god . . . Mama, we've got to walk to the hospital . . . you're really in bad shape . . . I'm scared you're gonna die." Then he grabbed me by the hand, and we started walking.

Finally another car came by, picked us up and brought us to the hospital.

That was almost a year ago. Now, thanks to Rocky pushing me up that hill, I'm alive. They told me I'd never have full use of my arms again, but they were wrong. I'm doing fine.

Rocky's put it all behind him, too. He's back to

playing sports and doing all the other things he does, like nothing ever happened. Right now, he can't make up his mind whether he wants to grow up to be a football player, like his daddy, or an artist!

Leatrice Harrison: Night Fire

It's a quiet February night in Greenwood, South Carolina. Ten-year-old Leatrice Harrison is spending the night at her grandmother's house, along with her three-year-old sister, Jametta, and two young cousins.

In the middle of the night, Leatrice awakens, catching a trace of smoke in the air. When she opens her bedroom door, heavy smoke pours in from the direction of the kitchen. Something in the kitchen had caught on fire, and the flames had spread so quickly that the entire room had been consumed. The entire house would be in flames in a matter of seconds.

Leatrice quickly wakes her baby sister. By now the smoke is so thick their eyes sting, and they can barely breathe. Keeping low to the ground, where the air is better, Leatrice tells Jametta to follow her, then rouses her cousins, bringing them through the smoke and out into the safety of the cool night.

By now the entire house is aflame. Windows shatter, walls buckle, sparks and huge cinders are cast into the sky by the force of the blaze . . .

. . . And that's when Leatrice realizes that Jametta isn't there. Jametta had been so scared that she hadn't followed her sister out of the house!

Leatrice races back into the burning building, and finds Jametta still in the bedroom, surrounded by flames. As Leatrice grabs Jametta, their clothes ignite, and Leatrice tries to protect her baby sister from the flames.

They barely escape from the inferno with their lives.

Both Leatrice and Jametta are hospitalized for second- and third-degree burns. Leatrice's burns are so bad that she has to stay in the hospital for almost a month, but in the end she and her sister recover from that awful night, thanks to Leatrice's fast action.

Newsflash!

WINONA, TEXAS—After one man lost consciousness trying to rescue a suffocating sewer worker trapped far below ground, sixteen-year-old Gregory Dickens selflessly descended into the deadly shaft to rescue both men, nearly losing his own life in the process.

Anthony Lamb was working to repair a sewer line when the oxygen in the shaft thinned and was replaced by noxious fumes. Morris Neeley, 49, descended into the shaft to rescue Lamb, but Neeley, too, was overcome, and passed out.

Thinking quickly, Greg grabbed a rope, entered the manhole, and descended the ladder. He attached the rope to Neeley, but lost consciousness before he could get out.

A chemical worker wearing protective gear was next to descend into the hole. He finished tying the rope around Neeley. People above pulled the man to the surface. Next they removed Gregory in the same manner, and finally Lamb.

Gregory and Morris Neeley recovered from the ordeal, but Anthony Lamb had been down there too long and had suffocated. Had Gregory Dickens not risked his life, Morris Neeley might not have been rescued in time.

Colleen Cooke: Trouble on the Trail

When you're in an emergency, it's important to keep calm, and not to panic. Colleen Cooke found herself in a crisis, far, far away from anyone who could help her. Here is her story:

My father and I like to go horseback riding. I'm not very experienced, but I do know how to ride. Last May we took a new trail that wound up a mountain. It took us three hours or so to get to the top—but as we got there, my horse stopped. He wouldn't go through some bushes. My dad got off his horse and tried to help. He was going around to get something out of his saddlebag when my horse kicked him in the face. He fell right to the ground.

I got off my horse. I was going to go for help, but I didn't want to leave my dad there. His whole head was bleeding pretty badly—especially around the eye that got kicked. Then Dad's horse ran away. It was cold, and there were patches of snow everywhere, because we were so high up. Thinking fast, I took some snow and put it on my dad's head to help ease the pain and stop the bleeding. When he felt a little better, we started to go down the mountain. We tried to ride my horse for a little while, but he couldn't—it hurt too much—so I walked with him. There were plenty of times I thought he wasn't going to make it. I was scared, so I kept trying to convince myself his cut wasn't really so bad, even though I knew it was.

Whenever he wanted to slow down and stop, I would tell him that it was going to rain, and Mom was gonna get worried, and stuff like that, to try to keep him moving all the time. It was a long trip down the mountain—it felt like it was never going to end.

My mom knew something was wrong even before we got back, because Dad's horse went straight home. She sent for my uncle.

We finally got Dad to the hospital, but it was so bad, they had to take him to an even bigger hospital—Eastern Idaho Regional Hospital.

They tried to save his eye, but they couldn't. He lost it. Still, it could have been a whole lot worse.

Newsflash!

SAN MANUEL, ARIZONA—Twelve-year-old Hector Sierra made an electrifying rescue today.

Hector was climbing a tree with his friend Andrew when all of a sudden Andrew slipped, lost his grip on a tree-limb, and began a twenty-foot fall.

Andrew reached for whatever he could get his hands on and found himself grabbing a live high-voltage wire! Hector reached out to grab his friend and save him, but when he did, Hector became the ground for the electrical current—that is, the electricity passed through Andrew and Hector, and into the tree.

Hector was able to break Andrew's fall and get him free from the wire, but both boys were rushed to the hospital, nearly electrocuted. Their condition was listed as serious.

Both boys survived. Since the incident last year, Hector has needed three operations to recover from the electrical burns he received, but the knowledge of having saved his friend's life has kept him cheerful and brave through it all.

Brent Meldrum
and the
"Time-Life Remover"

Susan Meldrum says her five-year-old son Brent is a very confident boy. She also says he's very strong for his age. Perhaps his strength and confidence comes from the karate classes he takes, but wherever they come from, they saved Tanya Branden's life!

Brent and Tanya were playing together when Tanya began to choke on a piece of hard candy.

"I heard about this thing called the 'Time-Life Remover,' or something like that," says Brent. "I saw it on this TV show called *Benson*. Benson was choking and this guy goes behind him, then puts both arms around him, squeezes him real hard, and saves him.

"I could see Tanya was turning blue—really blue. My mother was going crazy, yelling at me to get away, but I didn't listen, because I knew what I had to do. Tanya could barely talk, so I went behind her and gave her the Time-Life Remover—I squeezed and lifted her up. She weighed forty pounds, but I did it. Then I banged her down on her feet. Finally she coughed and the candy flew out. Tanya was really glad. She says I'm her hero. She didn't kiss me or anything, though. I mean, I'm just her boyfriend!"

What Brent did is not the Time-Life Remover, but the *Heimlich maneuver*, developed in 1974 by a man named Henry Heimlich. If someone is choking on a piece of food or other small object, the Heimlich maneuver can save his or her life. You put your arms around the victim from behind, clasping your hands together in front. Then with the lower knuckle of your thumb, you thrust sharply right beneath the rib cage. That will cause whatever is stuck in the victim's windpipe (or *trachea*) to pop out with a rush of air. It might not seem so difficult, but before the Heimlich maneuver was invented, many people choked to death because no one knew how to save them. Now thousands of people's lives are saved each year by the Heimlich maneuver—and it's so easy, even a five-year-old child can do it!

Brent's not the only kid who's saved someone with the Heimlich maneuver—Amy Barbee saved two people at a retirement center she worked at, and eight-year-old Freddie Self saved his friend's life.

"Now I'm this big hero," says Brent, who got a lot of publicity from his life-saving episode. "People just keep calling all day—the news and people like that. I wouldn't mind it so much, but they always call me in the middle of cartoons, you know?"

Newsflash!

LAMU, KENYA—Yesterday, Fatuma Dhidha, only six years old, saved her mother, Esha, from the angry jaws of a hungry crocodile.

Fatuma and her mother were getting water from a river on their island home of Lamu, when, out of nowhere, the crocodile leapt out and clamped down on the woman's arm. Fatuma distracted the crocodile with a shiny can. When the crocodile lunged after the can, Fatuma's mother broke free. The two of them ran away—and as anyone can tell you, running away is the best thing you can do if you're facing a hungry crocodile!

Being Prepared

Trevor Willson, 12, spends an afternoon with several friends cliff-diving off the rocks and into the cool Pacific Ocean, on California's Catalina Island. This ten-day trip to Catalina is supposed to be the highlight of the boys' summer—but today something goes horribly wrong.

As he waits his turn to dive, Trevor loses his footing on the slippery rock, plunging down the side of the cliff.

Had he fallen farther away from the rocks he might have been all right, but he is too close, and fifteen feet down, he crashes into an eighteen-inch outcrop of rock. He lands on his chest, stomach and arm, then falls ten more feet, splashing face down into the rough ocean.

Trevor Willson's life could have ended in tragedy, but the company he had chosen to keep saved him.

Instantly his friends Read Kerlin, 15, and Justin

Mueller, 14, swim out to Trevor, turn him over, elevate his head and chest, and shield him from the rocks.

Read swims to shore, holding Trevor in a "cross-chest carry," but a strong undertow keeps tugging at them. The powerful current threatens to drag them out to sea. Fighting the undertow, Read swims with all his strength, kicking with both feet and pulling the water with one arm; the other arm is hooked around Trevor's body. They inch toward the beach, and at last they are met halfway by lifeguards.

The paramedics are slow in coming, but on shore, five other teenagers calmly take control—five more of Trevor's friends. They give Trevor first aid, treating him for shock, and hold him down as he thrashes back and forth, screaming with pain.

Finally, an hour later, the paramedics arrive and take Trevor to the hospital.

He is found to have a partially collapsed lung, a concussion, and a broken wrist.

You might think it was one magnificent stroke of luck that all of Trevor's friends knew lifesaving techniques, but it was not luck at all. Trevor, Read, and Justin, as well as their friends on the beach, were all members of Boy Scout Troop 223—and Troop 223 is famous for being one of the nation's highest-achieving scout troops.

Two out of every five scouts who join the troop become Eagle Scouts—the highest honor in scouting. The national average is only two out of every hundred! Troop 223's record is twenty times better than the national average, and the troop has turned out 294 Eagle Scouts so far!

The boys attribute their success to their scoutmaster, Michael Lanning, a man who takes great pride in the boys, and treats them like family.

"Mike's philosophy is you don't lose," says Assistant Scoutmaster John R. Wilson. "If you're going to be a success in life, you don't lose, and you don't quit."

The seven scouts on the Catalina shore certainly didn't lose or quit that day when they pulled Trevor Willson from the Pacific surf. Now Trevor owes his life to his able-bodied friends of Troop 223—the Boy Scouts who proved once and for all what they really mean when they say, "Be prepared!"

Newsflash!

WEST SENECA, NEW YORK—Twelve-year-old James Bliemeister used quick thinking and even quicker gum chewing today to ward off a disaster.

James was baby-sitting at a neighbor's house when the three-year-old child he was staying with rammed his pedal fire engine into a gas pipe. Gas began to hiss out of a hole in the pipe. If James didn't stop the leak quickly, there could have been an explosion!

James remembered he had seen a pack of chewing gum upstairs. Holding his finger in the hole, he sent the three-year-old to get the gum, but the little boy didn't understand. He brought James some toy cars instead. James sent the boy off again. Finally the child returned with the gum. James popped several pieces into his mouth, chewing until the gum was soft enough, then used the wad to plug the hole. After he tied the gum in place with a sock,

James called his father, and his father called the gas company.

When the gas company arrived, James was commended for saving the day, and acting very responsibly in a dangerous situation.

Michelle Lampert: On an Icy Lake . . .

Eleven-year-old Michelle Lampert does not know how to swim. Of course, there are lots of people who can't swim, but how many nonswimmers do you know who have saved two people from drowning?

Cheney Lake is located on the eastern side of Anchorage, Alaska. It's a deep, icy lake with banks of thick mud.

Two boys were playing on a piece of land that jutted out into the lake. It took only a moment for them to lose their footing and find themselves up to their necks in water, sinking into mud as thick as tar.

The boys panicked and screamed at the top of their lungs for help. The only person to hear them was Michelle. By the time Michelle got to the scene, only one boy was screaming; the other was floating in the lake, unconscious. Michelle threw a rope to the conscious boy and dragged him to safety, but saving the other boy was not going to be as easy. He was floating face down, and had probably been sent into shock by the frigid forty-degree water of the lake. As far as Michelle knew, he was already dead.

Even though Michelle could not swim, she made her way out into the icy water. She grabbed the boy and pulled him toward shore, ignoring the sting of the water as it drained the heat from her shivering body.

Back on shore, Michelle pumped the boy's stomach, using a technique she had learned in school. Finally the boy coughed up water and began to breathe again.

Had it not been for Michelle's bravery, the two boys would have suffered an icy death in the cruel waters of Cheney Lake.

Newsflash!

ONTARIO, CALIFORNIA—On Christmas eve, ten-year-old John Lynch broke into a burning car and prevented what could have been a terrible tragedy.

While riding his bicycle, John saw a car that was filled with smoke—but worse, inside he could make out the outline of a small child.

He jumped off his bike and opened the car door. Inside, four-year-old Billy Parker was surrounded by fire, and choking on the smoke of the burning car. Billy liked to play with matches. He had been lighting them while alone in his mom's car, which was filled with clothes.

John quickly got Billy out of the car and brought him to John's grandmother's house, where they washed Billy's burns with cold water. Thanks to John, Billy's burns were not very serious, but he did have to spend three days in the hospital for smoke inhalation.

John, a fourth grader, was honored by the mayor, received the keys to the city, and got to meet the President.

Joseph Jackson:
An Impossible
Strength

People have been known to do amazing feats in emergency situations: average people have lifted entire automobiles to save someone's life, or carried several people at a time from a fire. Thirteen-year-old Joe Jackson found himself in a terrifying situation, and like many others, found strength he never knew he had. . . .

It happened like this . . . we were moving out to Virginia, and our Bronco was loaded right to the hilt with all of our possessions. I rode up front with Mom, and my cousin Billy rode in the very back, behind the backseat. Around him we had packed everything under the sun . . . I mean there were sleeping bags, lamps—the Bronco was packed solid. We were taking a shortcut to our new home, going down a narrow, winding gravel road. Lately we'd been having a lot of trouble with the Bronco—it would rev up real fast and then cut down, and then it would kick in real fast again without any warning.

Anyway, we were going about thirty miles an hour around this curve when the Bronco went out of control. We swerved to the other side of the road, came back, hit a bridge, and flew right off of the bridge, into the water.

The water was deep, because beavers had dammed up the river below. Mom's window was down, and as the car hit the water, we tipped, and water began to gush in. We were submerging fast! In a second, we were completely underwater. My mom, who can't swim, was choking and gasping as the water filled her lungs. That's when I rammed my fist through my window to break it. I pulled Mom over, and out the window—I don't know how I was able to do it, but I did. She was choking and coughing when we broke surface—completely out of it—and I swam with her to shore. The slippery embankment was steep, and it was hard to get her up there, but somehow it was like I suddenly had superhuman strength or something, and I pushed her up. I really don't know how I was able to do it!

It wasn't until now that I realized I had a deep gash on my wrist, and it was bleeding pretty badly. Then it dawned on me that my ten-year-old cousin Billy was still in the car, completely blocked in!

"I got to get Billy, I got to get Billy," I screamed and went back into the water, swimming toward the submerged car. I stuck my hand in the car, opened the door, and had to unpack the whole backseat to get to Billy—everything under the moon was stuffed in around him—I thought I'd never get to him. Finally I found him, carried him out, and brought him over to shore. He had a bad bruise, but he was okay.

My aunt, grandfather, and brother were up at the bridge. They'd been driving way ahead of us, but heard the crash and came back. Now that it was over, I was pretty shaky, and losing blood fast. My aunt came down, took off her blouse, and wrapped it around my wrist to stop the bleeding. Then they rushed us all over to the hospital. They stitched my wrist up all right, but because the water in that river was so dirty, I got a bad viral infection, and had a temperature of one hundred and four for two days.

When you think about it, it was really like a miracle that we all survived this thing. My mom says that I must have had an angel helping me there, giving me all that strength, and making everything go so well. Maybe she's right, but all I know is that I couldn't have lived if I didn't save my mother from that car.

Newsflash!

LITTLE ROCK, ARKANSAS—Brandy and Misty Penry, abducted from their parents over two years ago, were reunited with their parents yesterday, thanks to Angela Thornton, age eleven.

Angela, who worked at the school cafeteria, recognized Brandy from a missing-child photograph which had been mailed to her home. Angela recognized her right away. "I used to see her every day when the little girl would get her milk," Angela said.

Angela talked to her teacher, who in turn alerted authorities. After an investigation, the couple who had kidnapped the sisters were arrested, and the girls were returned to their parents.

For being so perceptive and reuniting the family, Angela was invited to Washington, D.C., to meet President Reagan.

Captive!

When Patrick Hood, 15, Raymond Smith, 16, and Michael Wissman, 17, were sent to the disciplinarian's office of the Archbishop Ryan High School for Boys, they didn't expect to be there for seven and a half hours. Nor did they expect to be held at gunpoint.

The ordeal began at 12:45 P.M., when a man by the name of Steven Gold walked into the disciplinarian's office.

"He was talking about politics and the President," said a witness. "He was just talking to anyone who would listen."

In the office along with the three boys were Dorothy Gay, the office secretary; Father Carl Graczyk, assistant dean of students; and David Hajduk, a fellow student, age 15. During his mad ravings, Gold pulled out a gun, closed the door, and announced that he was taking them all hostage. Police arrived at the scene in minutes.

The gunman insisted that a letter be delivered to the President. The letter demanded that the President step down from office and appoint him President. "Either choose my leadership," the letter said, "or accept the death of America." The letter went on to say that if the President did not step down, forces of evil would wreak havoc in America.

Gold was armed and dangerous, and neither Patrick, Raymond, nor Michael knew whether they would get out of that office alive. Neither the hostages nor the police could talk the gun out of Gold's hand. Finally Gold refused to allow any of the hostages to talk at all.

Almost twenty minutes into the ordeal, the gunman sent David Hajduk out to bring him something to drink—he was ordered to return or the remaining hostages would suffer. The police refused to let him go back in.

Now five hostages remained.

Outside the fence, crowds of people gathered while the police tried to negotiate with Gold. By five o'clock, he had released the secretary, and at seven o'clock, he released the priest, but he refused to release the three boys until his demands were met.

It was clear that his demands could never be met, and the police would have to break in. If that happened, the hostages might be killed.

The boys decided it was time for action!

Michael Wissman thought that the gun might be a starter pistol because the barrel of the gun was blocked—but he couldn't be sure. Besides, starter pistols can be used as .22-caliber weapons. The boys also knew that Gold had a knife, and perhaps other weapons, hidden beneath his long black overcoat.

Although the three boys were not allowed to talk to one another, through hand signals they were able to put together a plan to overcome their captor.

At eight-twenty that evening, the boys attacked. There was a struggle. The gunman screamed and aimed the gun. Michael wrestled the gun from his hands, and the other two boys found and took away the knife. Instantly police broke in and Gold was arrested.

Amanda Lawrence: A Birthday Story

Amanda Lawrence's mom and dad didn't plan on taking Amanda to their childbirth class, but that day they couldn't find a baby-sitter. It was a lucky thing, though, that seven-year-old Amanda did attend that class and saw a film on childbirth, because a few weeks later, Amanda had to help deliver her mom's baby!

At about seven-thirty on the morning of Edwin and Teri Lawrence's eighth wedding anniversary, just as Amanda was getting ready to go to school, Mrs. Lawrence went into labor. Amanda and her mom were alone in the house.

Mrs. Lawrence couldn't get to the phone to call for help, so Amanda dialed the operator, who connected her with the 911 emergency operator. With the aid of the emergency operator, Amanda helped her mother calm down. Then Amanda gave the operator directions to the Lawrences' house, which would be hard for an ambulance to find, since it was in a rural area outside of Atlanta, Georgia.

Usually, when a woman goes into labor, it takes several hours, or even an entire day, for the baby to be born—leaving plenty of time to get to a hospital. But it doesn't always work that way.

While Amanda was still on the phone, it became clear that the ambulance was not going to get to them in time. Here's a bit of the conversation between Amanda and the emergency operator:

AMANDA: *Momma's water broke . . .*
OPERATOR: *Is she all right?*
AMANDA: *She's all right.*
OPERATOR: *Is she crying?*
AMANDA: *No, she's breathing.*
OPERATOR: *Okay.*
AMANDA: *She's hardly breathing and the baby's coming . . . the baby's here. It's trying to breathe. The baby is blue. She doesn't know what to do for it. Are they almost here?*

Amanda stayed right by her mother as she delivered her baby boy herself. Once he was born, Amanda wrapped her baby brother in blankets to keep him warm. It had been less than twenty minutes since Amanda first called for help, and rescue workers didn't arrive for fifteen more minutes.

Everyone involved was amazed at how calmly Amanda had handled everything—from the phone call, to taking care of her mom during the delivery, to taking care of the baby afterward. The "one big problem" that had worried Amanda through the whole thing, as she had told the operator, was that they didn't know what to name the baby yet, since he was two weeks early.

They named the six-pound nine-ounce boy William Zachary Lawrence, and he and his mom were just fine when they got to the hospital.

"I was shocked, but I knew what was going on, even though he came out a little purplish, purple-blue," said Amanda, later that day. "I think I did a great job, and it was a good idea I helped little Zachary be born!"

Newsflash!

MARCUS HOOK, PENNSYLVANIA— Lawrence Weigand III saved the life of an eight-year-old girl today, in the nick of time.

Eight-year-old Judith McGrath was playing in the middle of the street—a street that was closed to traffic—when a car drove around the barricades at the end of the block. The car was speeding, and the driver was drunk.

When thirteen-year-old Lawrence saw the car approaching, he ran into the street and knocked the girl out of the speeding car's path. The car barely missed them, and drove on without so much as slowing down.

Kids to Remember

Performing a rescue usually means putting your own life at risk, and for almost every hero who successfully saves someone's life, there's one who dies trying.

It's important to remember how dangerous rescues can be. You should never try to perform a rescue unless you *absolutely have to* in order to save someone's life. Remember: If you're not a hero, it doesn't mean you're a coward. Sometimes there's nothing we can do to help someone. Sometimes our own safety has to come first.

Here's a list of courageous kids who should not be left out of this book. They are all heroes, and have won the Carnegie Hero Award, but these kids weren't as lucky as some others. They died in attempting their rescues.

* * *

Kristine E. Boring, 11

Drowned in a California river while attempting to rescue a girl older than her.

Kelli Lea Brooks, 13

Attempted to rescue a small child from the path of a speeding truck.

Mark Alan Foss, 14

Attempted a rescue in Lake Michigan.

David Paul Kastl, Jr., 17

Drowned in Lake Michigan after saving his sister, Diane.

Gershom McCaleb, 15

Attempted to rescue two young girls from a rough river.

Raymond Leonard Mills, 15

Drowned in a public pool while attempting to save his panicking brother, who was a nonswimmer.

Wade R. Nolan, 9

Dove off a bridge into a reservoir to rescue a younger boy.

Seldon Clark Pierce, 15

Attempted a water rescue off the coast of Nova Scotia.

Andrew T. Spence, 16

Drowned attempting to save a small boy who slipped into the ocean.

You may have noticed that all but one of these kids drowned, proving once and for all that water rescues are not as easy as they may look. Only exceptionally strong swimmers should attempt to save a drowning victim—especially when the water is rough or cold.

The Ultimate Gift

Here's a special kid to remember. A boy who saw beyond his own life, and knew that with his death, he could give a dying friend the gift of life—three whole years of it!

Fifteen-year-old Felipe Garza loved to break-dance. He would skillfully bounce around the floor, and spin on his head—but there was one girl who could make his head spin even when he wasn't break-dancing; fourteen-year-old Donna Ashlock.

Donna worked as a waitress at the Tiger's Den, a hamburger place where Felipe went to play video games. He would make her laugh by telling jokes and dancing to songs he would sing. They were really good friends but were not boyfriend and girlfriend.

Felipe came from a very poor family—the five of them lived in a one-bedroom converted motel room, and Felipe's bed was two blankets on the floor. His father, who could neither read nor write, couldn't find work, and the family lived on welfare.

When Donna and Felipe were in ninth grade, the first signs of Felipe's illness began to show. Felipe began to suffer from severe headaches and blackouts. Sometimes the pain was so great that he would have to take time off from school. He didn't want to tell anyone at school about being sick, and when it was clear to his friends that something was wrong, he would cover up by making jokes. He never let on how severe his illness was—not even to his family, because Felipe did not want the family to spend what little money they had to take him to the doctor.

Meanwhile, Donna was having problems of her own. A few weeks before Christmas, Donna started to have problems breathing and had stomach pains. Her parents rushed her to a local hospital where doctors first diagnosed her as having appendicitis— but the diagnosis was wrong. They were all shocked two days later when the tests showed she had *cardiomyopathy*—a degeneration of the heart muscle. Without a heart transplant, Donna would die in six to eight weeks.

When Felipe learned of Donna's disease, he startled his family by saying, "I'm going to die, so I can give my heart to Donna." His family did not pay much attention to his premonition because he seemed so healthy.

A few days later, Felipe complained of pain on the left side of his head. He walked into the bathroom, collapsed and never regained consciousness.

A blood vessel had burst inside his brain, and Felipe was gone even before his parents were able to get him to the hospital.

At the hospital, Felipe was put on a respirator. It was clear that he was not going to come out of this coma—he was "brain dead," but the respirator kept his body alive. It was then that his parents remembered how Felipe had wanted to give his heart to Donna. Since he was on the respirator, and his heart could be kept alive until the transplant could be performed, Felipe's parents chose to honor their son's wishes and donate his heart to Donna.

On Sunday, January 5, a five-hour operation put Felipe's heart into Donna's chest.

Three days after the operation, Donna's father, Raymond Ashlock, told Donna that Felipe had died, and that he had donated his eyes and kidneys to other people.

There was a pause.

"And I have his heart," Donna said quietly. She had guessed even before she'd been told.

A surprising number of remarkable events and coincidences had come together to enable Felipe to give Donna his heart. First he predicted his own death. Second, Felipe was blood type O, which made him a universal donor. Anyone can accept blood or internal organs from a type O donor. Third, both teenagers were approximately the same size and weight. Had Felipe been much bigger than Donna, his heart would have been too big. Fourth, the tissue compatibility tests performed before the surgery determined that Donna's body had an excellent chance of accepting Felipe's heart. And finally, timing played a very key role. Just before Donna's operation, her heart had deteriorated to such a level that she was in critical condition. Had Felipe lived even a little longer, Donna might have died waiting for a donor.

Almost five hundred people came to Felipe's funeral; family, friends, and people who did not even know him came to say good-bye to this caring young man.

While Donna could not leave her hospital room to attend the funeral, she said good-bye by having her father place a single red rose on the casket. Written on the ribbon tied to the stem was, "With Love, Donna Ashlock."

After any transplant operation there is always the fear the receiving body will reject the new organ, and a heart transplant is a tricky operation indeed.

Donna Ashlock lived over three years with Felipe's heart—over a hundred-and-ten-million beats. She grew into a fine young woman of seventeen before time finally caught up with her, and her body, no longer able to accept a heart that was not its own, rejected it, and Donna died.

Had it not been for Felipe, Donna would never have gotten those three years—three years that meant everything in the world to her.

SURVIVORS

Being a hero doesn't always mean rescuing someone else. Sometimes it means rescuing yourself from dark, lonely, and frightening situations.

Bad things can happen to good people. People can be hurt, get very sick, or be put through awful ordeals. When things like that happen to us, we have a choice: we can give up, or fight for our lives and overcome.

All the kids in this chapter have been in harsh situations. Some faced death, others faced fates worse than death, but all of them had the courage to fight for themselves, beating impossible odds.

We'll begin with a story of identical twin boys who, for five years, had to fend for themselves . . .

Just You and Me . . .

Most kids worry about things like grades and their allowance, but John and Tony Gomez's concerns go a little further than that. They've had to worry about rent and electric bills.

John and Tony are twins, born and raised in the United States. Their parents were divorced when the boys were young, and they lived with their father until they were thirteen. One day their father made a decision that would change the boys' lives. He decided to move back to Guadalajara, Mexico.

The boys resisted going with their father. After all, they'd been brought up in California, not Mexico, and they were afraid they would have to repeat their schooling if they left. They chose to stay in the United States.

It wasn't easy living alone. Not only did they have to pay all the bills, but they had to fool friends, neighbors, and school authorities—for if the authorities found out they were living alone, they might be sent out of the country, or even worse, they might be split up and sent to different homes.

At age thirteen, the twins began working at night, while still going to school during the day. They made sure to keep their grades up, so the school would never have a reason to call home. The twins even went to school when they were sick, for fear that if they were absent, the school would call home and find out that they were alone. Eventually they had their father bring them a stack of signed stationery so they could write school notes and excuses.

Their first job was at a bakery. They were too young for a real job, but their friend's father let them work anyway, never knowing that the twins' father was gone. Tony worked six days a week, while John studied a little more and worked a little less.

When friends and neighbors visited their house trailer and wondered where the boys' father was, the boys would make up stories. "Our father is on a business trip," they would say, or "He's on vacation." At first their father came back once a month, but soon his visits became fewer and further between.

Even with the boys working, paying the bills became next to impossible. There were electric bills, phone bills, and the rent to pay, not to mention food. It was too much to handle. The resourceful twins ate free lunches at school and free dinners at work to keep down the grocery bill. They scrimped and saved, building bicycles from old parts rather than buying them, denying themselves simple things like birthday and Christmas gifts, because there simply wasn't any money for that.

John and Tony lived this way for three years. When they were sixteen, they finally told their best friend that they were living alone. Their friend's family took them in for a year, and the twins started saving money. By then they were working for fast-food chains. They would work from five in the afternoon to midnight, or even to one in the morning, staying up all night long to study for exams. Still, they kept their secret from almost everyone.

At seventeen, John and Tony moved into a small apartment of their own, in a low-rent area. John worked his way up to supervisor of a neighborhood Del Taco.

Now the twins are eighteen, and have finally let people know that they have been alone, living by their wits and hard work, for the past five years. In spite of the long hours of work to pay the bills, they both have graduated from high school.

Tony plans to join the Navy and go to college when he is discharged in four years. John is determined to go to college right away, and although the money isn't there yet, he's determined to work it out. John has already begun taking college classes with the help of donations from friends and concerned citizens.

Segura Williams
Looks for a Home

If you ever think your room is too small, or are up in arms because you have to share your room with a brother or sister, you might want to think of Segura Williams. Thirteen-year-old Segura doesn't share a room with a brother or sister. He doesn't have a room to share.

Segura is one of thousands of homeless people who live in the streets of this country. Segura and his mother and nine brothers and sisters live in a tent in Los Angeles. Their tent is in a special campground for homeless people.

Segura couldn't stand being ignored by the city's government, and so he single-handedly took up his case with the Los Angeles City Council.

"We need so much help," pleaded Segura, "and this problem is not going to go away unless we do something about it. We kids can make a difference. We want to help our families get out of here and into permanent houses."

His plea was heard by the mayor of Los Angeles, who said he would personally visit the campsite to speak with Segura and his friends.

Segura has now organized a group called Kids Helping Each Other. He and his friends collect food, money, and clothes for the people of the camp. The group has even organized a daily breakfast.

Segura's hope and strength in the face of homelessness is something to be proud of, and something we can all learn from.

The Courage of
Sage Volkman

I love you, Sage, so very much, please hang in there with us. Six days have gone by since the accident. This is the first day I have been able to write about you or what has happened. I, as your mother, am doing this for you because it is my legacy to you. You will be forever changed by what has happened and have a right to know about this time in your life when your energy is being used to help heal your body and you are in a doorway to a dream. I will give this to you when you are ready: when you ask to know how it was.*

That note was written by six-year-old Sage Volkman's mom when Sage was in the hospital. No one knew if Sage would survive the third- and fourth-degree burns she had all over her body—but

*Klein, Julie. "A Courage Beyond Understanding," *People Weekly*, March 21, 1988, p. 28.

Sage did survive, and her story of courage is an inspiration for grown-ups as well as kids. Sage Volkman is truly a hero!

It was a bright day in October when it happened. Mr. Volkman was camping with Sage and her younger brother Avery. While Mr. Volkman and Avery went out early to fish, Sage slept late. Sometime later, Mr. Volkman saw some smoke in the distance, and he realized it was coming from the direction of their camper. He raced back and found the camper ablaze—a cinder from the camper's wood-burning stove had set it on fire. Sage was nowhere to be seen.

Mr. Volkman kicked open the door and hurried in to save his daughter. He found her where he had left her, in her sleeping bag—which was already melting. Sage was on fire. He jumped from the camper with Sage just seconds before the entire camper exploded.

Sage was limp and barely alive, so Mr. Volkman pumped on her chest until he was sure she was breathing again. Sage was rushed to the hospital.

The news was not good.

Sage was burned so badly she had lost both hands, an ear, and her nose. Her face was burned beyond recognition. Her legs were burned so badly that no one knew if she would walk again—or if she would even survive.

Many people who are burned that badly don't pull through, but Sage had a strong will to live. She stayed in the hospital for two months. During her

stay, her skin and body slowly—very slowly—
began to heal. She needed many operations. Most
were skin grafts—the doctors took healthy skin
from unburned parts of her body and used it to re-
place the skin that was lost.

When someone is badly burned, there are many
things to worry about. There can be infection, and
illness. Sage almost died of pneumonia.

To help her heal and get well, Sage was given
hot baths. Her bandages were replaced more than
once a day. Every movement was so painful that
she had to be injected with a powerful painkiller
before the nurses could work on her.

Still, through the pain, Sage learned to hope. She
saw other kids who had been burned walk out of
the hospital, so she simply told herself that she
would be next.

All through her hospital stay, no one would let
Sage see her own face. Finally, when she was released, her parents let her see her reflection. The
face in the mirror was far better than it had been
the day of the fire, but there's only so much that
surgery can do.

Sage accepted it with a shrug. "Oh well," she
said. Outside she was no longer what she was before the fire, but what counted was what was inside, and that hadn't changed.

At home, Sage still had far to go. There were
more operations. As her skin healed, it would
shrink, and the slightest movement would cause her
terrible pain, but Sage gritted her teeth and went
through the necessary rehabilitation program,

slowly got her muscles and skin into proper shape. Sage was taught to use a special device: a prosthetic—or artificial—hand. She learned how to write and draw with it in only six months.

Now Sage is back in school. She's an above-average student in spite of her disabilities.

At first it was hard for her. Sage's classmates stared at her scarred face, and their mouths would drop open in shock, but soon her friends accepted her and things got back to normal.

In public it's not so easy. People stare at her in supermarkets and malls and other public places. Once a little girl took one look at Sage, screamed, and ran away—but Sage can live with that. "After all," says Sage, "if people stare or run away, that's their problem, not mine."

Sage's journey is not over. She'll need more operations as she grows older, but Sage has bright and glorious hopes for her future. Sage Volkman wants to be a doctor. With her strength, courage and determination, she'll certainly go as far as she dreams!

Pham Hong and the Meaning of Freedom

Pham Hong, twelve years old, won an essay contest with her entry, "What Freedom Means to Me." To Pham, freedom means an awful lot. Pham is Vietnamese, and she and her mother fought long and hard to get to the United States.

The trip began in Saigon, Vietnam. Mother and daughter walked out of the crippled city. There were soldiers to fight off. There were land mines buried in the forests they snuck through. They walked by night with bare, bloody feet. By day they would sleep, never knowing if they would be killed before they awoke, as were many other unfortunate people, whose bodies they found along the way.

After a year of walking, a short, secret boat trip landed them in Taiwan, and from there, Pham and her mom came to the United States.

For Pham Hong, freedom is something to hold dear—for she fought so long and hard to find it.

The Right Track

Charla Ramsey and Sacajuwea Hunter are the best of friends. For ten years they've been training together under the caring leadership of their coach Bill Greene, and they've seen some amazing results. In fact, at the age of fourteen, Sacajuwea was the youngest member of the U.S. Olympic team, and made a place for herself in the record books as the fourth fastest in the world in her events.

Pretty good, considering the fact that Sacajuwea Hunter lost both legs when she was a baby.

Charla tells of some experiences in their very noble sport. . . .

I first got involved in wheelchair racing when I was seven years old. An elementary school counselor got me interested. At first he'd asked me to be the mascot for his basketball team, and I said yes, because I'd get to travel. The next year he asked if I'd be interested in going out for track. That sounded really fun to me, so I joined the team, and I've been wheelchair racing ever since.

I met Saca that year in school, and we became good friends. She was a year younger than me, and she was really into sports too. We train together, but we don't race the same races, for several reasons. First of all, Saca is a distance racer, and I'm a sprinter. Secondly, we're not in the same class: she's a class five, and I'm a class four. Class depends on your level of disability. Anybody who is an amputee and could walk with artificial limbs is class five. Class four contains people with injuries to their lower spine, who have some movement in their legs and some stomach muscles. The lower the number, the less movement a person has, until you get down to classes 1a, 1b, and 1c, which represent quadriplegics—people who have paralysis of all four limbs.

Saca lost her legs when she was a baby. Her mother had put her in a tub of scalding water, and her legs were burned so badly that they couldn't be saved. After that, the courts took Saca away from her mother, because she couldn't care for Saca properly. When Saca was seven she was adopted by the Hunter family.

I have legs, but I was born with spina bifida—a malformed spinal column.

Now we're members of the Capitol Wheelchair Athletic Club in Washington, D.C. Currently there are five athletes on our track team. We train three days a week on the track and two days a week at a park, for about two or three hours a day—either in the morning or after school. We have weight training every other day.

We have a great coach—Bill Greene. Bill knows a lot about training, and he really has his heart in what he's doing. He enjoys it, and that's important.

Bill is also disabled. He had a gunshot wound in his spine. I don't think there's anyone more qualified to train wheelchair racers.

The wheelchairs we use for racing are not like everyday wheelchairs; those are basketball wheelchairs—they're more sturdy, heavier, and have smaller caster wheels, which enable you to turn quickly so you can get the ball. A racing wheelchair has bigger front casters, which help prevent vibration. The back wheels are thinner and are twenty-six inches wide, with special racing tires. Racing chairs are also very light—under twelve pounds, I believe.

Saca and I started winning important races when we were very young. In 1982 I was thirteen, and the youngest person to ever make the U.S. team. You had to run certain qualifying times to get on the team, and I made it! We went to London and to Nova Scotia to compete in the international games.

In England I got to race my first 1,500 meters. I was scared, because it was four laps, and since I'm a sprinter, I had never pushed four laps before. I said, "Oh no . . . I know I'm going to die up there," and everybody just kept telling me to pace it, and not push myself too hard at the beginning.

When the race began, everyone thought that I

ad gone out too fast, and I wouldn't be able to
eep that fast pace—but I maintained it. Then,
vhen it came down to the last one hundred meters,
 sprinted, and everyone was amazed because they
lidn't think I was going to have enough energy to
print. I ended up winning that race.

A couple of years later, Saca had her chance to
hine. We had been training hard for the '84 Olym-
ics, and we went together to the International
james in New York, which were the Olympic tri-
ls. I went to be with Saca, but I didn't compete.

The women competing there were from all over
he world. The American team had to be cut—only
he best racers would make the Olympic team. Saca
nade the top eight, and in the final race she took
hird place and was able to go to the Olympics.

She went to the Los Angeles Olympics with Bill,
nd took fourth place, making her the fourth-fastest
ong-distance wheelchair racer in the world, and the
hird fastest in the United States. She was also the
nly female amputee on the U.S. team, and the youn-
est member of the team as well, at fourteen.

Saca's favorite race was the one in New York,
vhen she qualified for the Olympics, but my favor-
te was the time I raced the 100 meters in Pennsyl-
ania. You see, I was competing against a woman
amed Sharon Hedrick, who is the fastest woman
n the world in class four. I have always looked up
o her, because she's so devastating on the track. In
he 100-meter race, I led for about seventy meters,
hen she caught up to me and won, but it was so
xciting racing with her—I felt that I could have al-

most gotten her if I was a little bit stronger and had more experience, you know? She's twenty-seven, and has had lots of years of training.

Now they're comparing me to her, and that's exciting, because she is the world's fastest woman.

As for the 1988 Olympics, well, we didn't make it this time around. Saca got sick, and couldn't keep up her training, and things just didn't work out for me, but we're already training for 1992.

I know I can still make it, because I'm still winning races all the time—last year I went to Paris, France, and I won the 100 meters at the World Championship Games, making me the fastest in the 100 meters in the world, so I'm really hopeful for 1992!

We both really love what we're doing, and I think that's important. I think that if you don't enjoy what you're doing, then you really don't benefit from it. We plan to keep racing for a long time!

Jason's Book
for Kids with
"Cansur"

Jason Gaes and his uncle, Terry, were playing with a magnifying flashlight one night.

"Open your mouth and I'll check for cavities," Terry said. Although he was checking for cavities, he found something else. He found a strange bump in Jason's mouth.

The next day a dentist sent Jason to see a surgeon, and the surgeon did some tests on Jason. Pretty soon Jason discovered another lump—this one on his stomach. It was growing fast—in one day the lump grew from the size of a golf ball to the size of a grapefruit.

Jason had Burkitt's lymphoma, a very deadly form of cancer. Jason was six, and the doctors didn't think he'd live to see seven. He would probably die in less than three months.

The next morning at 4:00 A.M. Jason began chemotherapy—medication to kill the cancer. He also had radiation therapy. The radiation made Jason lose his hair, and the chemotherapy made him feel sick, but it was the only way to kill the tumors that were growing all over his body.

For almost two years Jason was treated for the cancer, and slowly the cancer began to go away. While he was going through the therapy he and his mom read a book by another boy who had cancer. The boy had died before he finished writing it— someone else had to finish it. That made Jason angry, because it gave kids the impression that everyone with cancer has to die.

Jason decided to write a book for kids who were going through the same thing he was. Jason wrote, while his identical twin brother Tim and an older brother Adam drew pictures, and before long they had a book that Jason called *My Book for Kids with Cansur*. Maybe there were some problems with spelling, but everyone who read it knew that the words came from the heart.

Pretty soon a publisher decided to sell it as a real book. Here's some of what Jason had to say about cancer, in his own words:

> *I want to tell you kids don't always die. If you get cansur don't be scared cause lots of people get over having cansur and grow up without dying. Like Mike Nelson and Doug Cerny and Vince Varpness and President Reagan and me.*
>
> *Having cansur isn't fun. In fact it's the pits, but it's not all bad either. You get lots of cards and presents when your in the hospital.*
>
> *If you can find it, get a poster that says, "Help*

*me to remember, Lord, that nothing is gonna
happen today that you and me can't handle together." Then hang it in your room and read it at
night when your scared. If you get scared and
can't quit, go and talk to your Mom and she can
rock you or rub your hair.*

*Sometimes even if you do everything . . . a
pees of your cansur can break off and go to your
lungs and grow there. If the doctors can't get it
out then your probly gonna die when you're a
kid. My Mom said when me and Tim was babys
in her stumick we liked it in there . . . She says
heaven is probly like that. Once we get there we
won't want to come back here. We're just scared
about going to heaven because we never been
there.*

*Sometimes when your sick from a treatment
you miss school, but try to make up your work
cause colij makes you have all your work done
before you can be a doctor, and I'm going to be
a doctor who takes care of kids with cansur so I
can tell them what it's like.*

Jason recovered completely from his cancer. His
hair grew back, and everything's back to normal.
He likes sports—everything from swimming to
basketball—and his favorite football team is the
Miami Dolphins.

Jason's book was—and still is—a huge success.
He gets thousands of letters from kids who have
cancer, and even kids who don't. He's been on tele-

vision, and he's the subject of an Oscar-winning documentary film. . . .

. . . And Jason still wants to be a doctor, so that he can help young cancer patients.

My Book for Kids with Cansur: A Child's Autobiography of Hope, is available for $11.95 plus $1.50 for shipping from Melius & Peterson Publishing, Box 925, Aberdeen, SD 57402.

Laurinda Mulhaupt: Racing in the Dark

Being a star in both track and soccer at a competitive high school is not easy, but if you were to watch seventeen-year-old Laurinda Mulhaupt on the field or on the track, you'd see how easy she makes it look. She's a natural athlete, with all the right moves, and lots of determination.

One more thing . . .

. . . Laurinda is legally blind. . . .

It's called Stargardt's—the disease I have. It's very rare, and there's no corrective surgery. I didn't notice it until I was twelve—when my eyesight started getting worse. Now I'm seventeen and have 20/200 vision in both eyes. That's legally blind.

I didn't tell anybody because I didn't want to be treated differently. In school, I would cover up by sitting at the front of the classroom and holding books close when I read. If I still couldn't see, then I would get notes from friends. People really didn't think much about it, they just thought that I needed glasses.

In schools, especially high school, the teachers are supposed to be notified if a student has a problem like this. I figured all my teachers would know—but not all of them did. Sometimes they just didn't look at the records!

I was always into sports from the time I was very little. I like skiing, waterskiing, biking, tennis, soccer and track—and I was determined not to let my eyesight affect my performance. The only sport that I began to have a harder time with was tennis, but I can still play very well because I started playing before I began to lose my eyesight. If I had started later, I'd never have gotten anywhere.

I didn't start telling people about being legally blind until I was interviewed by the *Los Angeles Times*. I was doing very well in soccer—so well that the newspaper wanted to do an article on me. I spoke to my parents, and we agreed to do the article, and also to tell them about my eyesight—the newspaper didn't know a thing about it! Well, of course, that became an important part of the article.

Afterward, people who knew me were just so amazed, because they'd had no idea! Good friends would come up to me and would stand right in front of me and say, "Do you know who I am? What color are my eyes?" They were kidding, of course, but then they would ask why I never told them. I would answer by saying, "Well, you never asked!"

After the article, I started to get lots of letters.

People would write: "I have Stargardt's disease, too, and you're an inspiration to me," and things like that. I try to answer all the letters that I can. I love getting letters. I mean, who wouldn't love all that stuff.

As far as sports go, I'm going to continue playing. I've decided to focus on track more than the others. There's more of a future in it for me. My best races are the 800- and 1,600-meter relays.

My family has been great through all of this. I would have to say that the best thing in my life is my family. My dad says that I do too many things and I should take things slower—do them in proportion, and get my priorities straight. But, you know, I like getting involved in as many things as I can, and doing really well in them.

The Ordeal of
Ryan White

If you were to see Ryan White at a pizza place with his friends, you wouldn't notice anything different about him. He laughs, and smiles, and has as much fun as anyone. Perhaps more.

Looking at Ryan, you would never guess what he's been through, and what he's overcome. You'd never know that he was chased from his hometown of Kokomo, Indiana, by the fear and anger of the townspeople—as if he were Frankenstein's monster being chased by the ignorant villagers—but Ryan is no monster: Ryan is perhaps one of the most courageous boys in the world.

You see Ryan and his family were run out of town because of a disease. Ryan has AIDS.

Ryan was born in Kokomo, Indiana, and when he was still a little kid his parents learned that Ryan had hemophilia.

Hemophilia is a disease which keeps blood from clotting, or forming scabs. It might not sound too bad, but if a hemophiliac gets a scratch or a pin-prick, he or she could bleed to death!

All hemophiliacs need to be injected regularly with something called "clotting factor"—which is what hemophiliacs' blood is missing. Clotting factor enables hemophiliacs' blood to clot.

Ryan's life was pretty normal—until he got a bad batch of clotting factor. That's how he got AIDS.

You see, you can't get AIDS from touching something, or someone . . . You can only get it from body fluids like blood, and clotting factor comes from other people's blood.

Nowadays they have better ways of finding the bad blood before anyone can use it, but that was too late for Ryan.

When Ryan's family found out that Ryan had AIDS, Ryan's mom expected he'd have six months to live, but Ryan had his own ideas about that.

People in Kokomo were afraid of Ryan. Parents didn't want Ryan going to school: "Keep him away from my kids," parents would say. Ryan could not pass AIDS on to his classmates just by sitting with them, and breathing the same air, but people were still afraid.

"People would back away from me in the streets," Ryan said. "They'd run from me."

The school board was under so much pressure that they told Ryan he couldn't go to school any-more. His mom sued the school district to get Ryan back in school.

At that time, Ryan was pretty sick. He had lost weight—he weighed only fifty-four pounds. He was always shivering. Lots of celebrities had heard of Ryan's plight, and gave him their support—people like Tom Cruise, Charlie Sheen, Brooke Shields and Olympic diving superstar Greg Louganis. Elton John flew the whole family to Disneyland, and writes or calls Ryan every week!

Still, Ryan's health continued to get worse. At one point he almost died of pneumonia. He was given only a few more months to live.

Things in Kokomo were getting worse. Although they won the lawsuit allowing Ryan to go back to school, the White family wanted to move. One day Mrs. White went outside to find all her tires had been slashed, and that her car had been hit with dozens of eggs. People wrote awful things on Ryan's locker in school.

The last straw came one night, when out of nowhere someone fired a bullet through their living room window.

Ryan, his mom, and his sister Andrea moved to a town called Cicero. Although it was only twenty-five miles away from Kokomo, it was like a different world.

When they moved in, all their new neighbors welcomed them with open arms, and so did Ryan's new school.

Now, in a town that cared about him, Ryan's health began to change. He stopped getting chills, he became stronger, and he gained weight. Now, almost four years after getting AIDS, Ryan White is doing better than ever, has lived longer and been stronger than anyone believed possible. He's an A student again, and he's back to skateboarding and playing sports, although people tell him that he shouldn't.

Ryan's mere survival is enough to make him a hero—but his story doesn't stop here.

Ryan has gone around the country giving talks explaining to kids—and adults—everywhere the truth about AIDS, and sharing with people his joy of life. "I enjoy speaking with kids more than adults," Ryan says, "because kids listen."

People are amazed at how well Ryan handles everything—but Ryan goes on day to day, living life to the fullest. "It's how you live your life that counts," says Ryan. Ryan's friends say that he's the happiest person they know.

Ryan feels that his strength comes from his strong beliefs. "I have no fears now," he says, "I have a lot of trust in God." He knows that his faith and his love for life keep him going.

"If I were worried about dying, I'd die," Ryan says, "but I'm just not ready yet. I want to go to Indiana University."

Ryan White finally lost his long battle with AIDS in the spring of 1990, but the legacy of hope and courage he left behind will always be a source of inspiration to others suffering from AIDS—adults and children alike. In the short time he had, his messages about life and understanding touched the world. We could all learn a lot from Ryan White.

ACHIEVERS

So far we've talked about heroes of chance: kids who were thrown into difficult situations and came through with flying colors . . . but there's another kind of hero as well.

I'm talking about kids who, through their own determination, have accomplished something remarkable, or have given of themselves when other kids might have turned away.

Most of them aren't "super-kids"; they began with the same raw materials as everyone else—a brain and a desire to learn. It's what these kids chose to do that qualifies them as heroes.

Olympic athletes, young inventors, junior diplomats, and pint-sized adventurers: they're all here— kids who took their dreams and molded them into reality.

We'll begin with the adventure of a nine-year-old boy whose sky-high dream landed him a place in history.

Tony Aliengena: The Boy Who Could Fly

While most kids are out skateboarding o
playing video games, or just hanging around, Ton
Aliengena is ten thousand feet above the ground
behind the controls of a Cessna Centurion 210 air
plane, preparing for his flight across the country
Lots of pilots have flown from coast to coast in pri
vate planes, but Tony is a very special pilot. Yo
see, Tony is only nine years old.

Here's what Tony has to say about flying.

My dad's a pilot—he's been flying for aroun
fifteen years now. The earliest memory I have c
flying with my dad was when I was very, ver
young. I would fall asleep in the back of the plane
Lots of times I would get airsick, so to keep m
from getting sick, my dad would take me to th
front of the plane and sit me down on his lap. I wa
only a few years old when he gave me the control
I got to take off!

When I was four, he let me land the plane for the first time. Dad kept us straight with the rudders, and I actually landed. I learned pretty quickly that taking off and landing are the easiest parts of flying—those parts aren't as hard as you might think.

I never thought about breaking any records or anything, but then I saw this kid on TV. His name was Christopher Lee Marshall, and he had flown a plane across the country. He set a record for being the youngest ever to do it, and I was younger than him. I knew if I learned how to fly—I mean *really* fly—I could break his record.

I asked my dad if I could try, but my dad said no. A month later I asked him again. He must have realized it was something I really wanted to do, so he said I could.

He sat me down and we had a really serious talk about it. We looked at a calendar, and figured out just what it would take. We discussed all the time involved and problems that could arise—like if I got airsick.

My dad and I made an agreement. "Once you start," he told me, "you're going all the way." He wanted to make sure I was really determined to do it before we began. I agreed. Of course, he'd let me out of it if he thought safety was a problem, or if he thought I wasn't ready for the flight, but I couldn't just change my mind in the middle. That was okay, because I wasn't going to change my mind!

I knew it was going to take months and months

of hard work. No more skateboarding, no more watching TV shows, no more playing Nintendo for a while. I'd have to give all that time to flying with my instructor, Ed Fernett, every day after school. Sure, I wasn't going to have much time to play sports and stuff, but if I broke the record, that would be worth it!

I started my training, and began to learn. I had to have forty hours of flight time. My dad says I'm a born pilot. He says I pick things up very quickly.

I guess I'm a fast learner—I do well in school, even though I got held back in first grade. You see, I had problems learning to read—I couldn't move my eyes from left to right, and train them to move across the page. So I got held back for a year—but two years later, here I am flying a plane!

A typical day of flight training begins with the checklist. It's really important to check your instruments, your engine, your propeller cycle, and your mixture and fuel flow. Stuff like that. Then, once I'm up in the air with my instructor, I spend most of the time navigating from VOR to VOR. A VOR is a vortex omnirange—they're like landmarks. They look like big white upside-down cones, about twenty feet high, and you use the radio signals from the VORs to figure out where you are, and to navigate the plane. You fly from one VOR to another VOR, and practice navigating. I might fly out to Palm Springs, then to Orange County, and then to Oceanside.

Navigating—figuring out where you are and what direction you're going—is the hardest part of flying. You have to learn how to use maps really well, and practice navigating between VORs. If you're not good at navigating, you can really run into problems. For instance, when you're flying over clouds, and you can't see where you are, you really need to concentrate. You might think you're going over the ocean, but then you look at your VOR and you say, "That's impossible, I'm over land." You don't want to be lost above the clouds!

Sometimes I do get lost—my dad will sometimes get me lost on purpose, just so that I can learn how to find where I am. He'll shut the engine off on purpose, too, just so I know what to do, and how to start it—so I can get used to emergency situations. That's important. I wouldn't want to freak out while I'm up there.

Sometimes while I'm flying, my mind wanders. I might start thinking about what I'm going to do after I land, and I end up missing a VOR and getting lost. You really have to pay attention.

Flying's not really hard—not when you know what to do. It's harder than driving, I guess, because there are so many more instruments. And in a car you don't have VORs and stuff like that. It's about as hard as waterskiing on one ski—at least for me, because it took me a while to learn how to do that. One thing's for sure: flying's easier than English class!

Some kids at school didn't like what I was doing. They were jealous, I guess. They would call me names like "the Navigator," and I didn't like it that much. I just ignored them.

* * *

All this training was to prepare me for my cross-country flight. I wouldn't be alone in the plane for that, but I also wanted to set the record for being the youngest pilot ever to fly solo—that is, on my own, without anyone else in the plane.

Setting up the solo flight was not easy. I wanted to do my flight out of Oceanside Airport—that's the airport I'm used to, where I did all my flight training. The airport wasn't going to let me do it, so we petitioned the mayor. We went for a big meeting with the mayor, the city council, the airport manager, and some other people. Finally, they agreed to allow me to solo.

We were gonna have people from the news and from TV at my solo flight, but my parents weren't about to have me solo for the first time in front of all those reporters. I soloed unofficially a few weeks before.

I couldn't solo in the Cessna because I had to be sixteen to be allowed to fly it alone. That's an FAA rule. Ultralight planes are different, though. The FAA couldn't stop me from soloing in an ultralight plane.

The plane I flew is called the Eipper Quicksilver GT. I love flying the ultralight, because it's like a big toy. It's small, and it's lots of fun to fly. But on my first solo flight, I was a little scared. I remember I got out there on the runway. I look over and my father's not there, I'm all alone. I get to the end of the runway, and I say a little prayer.

And then I think to myself . . . I don't have to do

this if I don't want to. Thinking about that made me feel better, because I realized that I really wanted to. I took off and unofficially became the youngest person ever to solo in a plane!

Finally it was time for the official flight. My parents didn't get much sleep that night, but I did. We drove to the airport early, and I checked the plane. It was ready for flight. Lots of friends showed up, and we started talking. Lots of other people came too—the press and everything. They asked me questions and stuff. Finally it came time to make the flight. I was excited, but not too scared, because I had done it already. With everybody watching, I took off, did a touch-and-go (that's touching down for a second and taking off again) and flew the pattern. Now it was official! I was the world's youngest solo flyer, beating the record of a kid named Cody A. Locke, who was twenty-one days older than I was when he did it!

That's only half of it though. I still have to make my cross-country flight. I won't be alone for that. Ed—my instructor—is coming along. I'm glad that Ed's coming with me cross-country. I wouldn't want to go all by myself, I could get lost and wind up in Canada or something!

The big flight is only a few weeks away now. My training has gotten real intensive because while I'm in the air, I just can't make mistakes.

I'm a little worried about the weather—taking off through clouds is a breeze, but coming down through clouds isn't as easy. You can really get stuck if you have to stay IFR—that means you can't see, and you have to rely completely on your instruments when you're coming down. It's called an IFR approach.

Actually, I can do that okay—I *learned* to fly IFR. You see, I was small, and I couldn't see out the dash, so I had to learn how to land by using instruments. Still, it's scary. When you can't see where you are, you can roll the plane upside down, and it only takes a second to roll upside down like that! I just hope the conditions don't get too rough when I'm up there.

My dad says that once I cross the Rockies, the clouds never get above five thousand feet, so I'll be above them for most of the way. Still, it's gonna take at least four days to fly to the East Coast, and it's not gonna be easy. Now that it's really about to happen, my dad's giving me every chance in the world to back out, but I won't back out now. I'm gonna do it! I can hardly wait until I'm there and can spend a few days with my grandparents in Massachusetts!

TONY'S FLIGHT

The TV crews are waiting for Tony on the morning of his big flight. It is Easter vacation; a time for his classmates to relax and take a break from the third grade—but this third grader is anything but relaxed.

Tony packs a light bag, says a few words for the

reporters, and leaves with his family for southern California's John Wayne Airport.

The plane, a Cessna Centurion 216 propeller plane, is nothing like a big jetliner, but is a fine private plane. It is in the Cessna that Tony will attempt to make his record-breaking journey. Gathered at the airport are more than fifty people—reporters, family, and friends, all there to watch him begin his record-breaking flight.

Aboard the plane are Ed Fernett (Tony's instructor), a reporter, a photographer, and an observer from the National Aeronautic Association. The observer is there to make Tony's trip official. Tony calmly checks his instruments, and when he is satisfied that everything is flight-ready, Tony turns to his dad.

"Go show the world how to do it!" says Tony's dad, and with that, Tony snaps the plane's window closed. One wave to the TV cameras, and Tony is off on the first leg of his flight, sitting on a child's car seat so that he can see over the dashboard.

Tony's trip east should take three days, flying three to five hours each day.

The three-and-a-half-hour trip to El Paso, Texas, is a piece of cake, but as the small plane approaches the runway it is hit by fifteen-mile-per-hour crosswinds. Holding the controls tightly, Tony brings the Cessna in for a safe, but bumpy, landing.

After dinner Tony spends the night studying maps, preparing for the next day's flight to Dallas and Memphis, Tennessee.

On the following day, Tony makes it to Dallas

and Memphis with no problems. On his way into Memphis, the air traffic controllers hear his voice announcing his approach, and think it's a joke. A kid flying a plane? Tony guides the plane in for a soft landing. Now two-thirds of the country are behind him, and one-third remains . . . but that one-third may not be as easy as the first two. Weather reports for tomorrow's flight are not encouraging. Tony is going to have to fly through wild winds and heavy storms.

The next morning, with storm clouds threatening, Tony lifts off, leaving Memphis behind, but as he crosses over northern Alabama, the winds begin to toss the plane across the skies. The clouds grow denser and darker before him.

As if this is not enough trouble, all at once, an old problem comes rushing back.

Tony's airsickness.

Tony begins to rub his head and starts swallowing, trying to keep himself from getting sick and losing control of the plane.

The wind grows stronger; ice begins to form on the wings. It all becomes too much, and Ed, Tony's instructor, has to take control of the plane. Although he controls the plane for only about two minutes, Tony has to fly all the way back to Memphis and begin this leg of the flight again. If he doesn't, then he is disqualified; he must make the flight without anyone's help.

On the ground once more in Memphis, Tony fights his airsickness. He calls his parents, who are already waiting for him in Massachusetts. Once off the phone, he pops in a piece of gum, and starts thinking about what to do next. Dejected and disappointed, he sits with his head in his hands. The weather report for tomorrow is no better than today. He can't give up now! He just can't!

The air traffic controllers who guided him into Memphis cheer him up by inviting him to the tower. They have all been eager to meet the boy who could fly!

The next day, Tony takes off into the dark clouds once more, heading toward Richmond, Virginia. As soon as he hits five thousand feet, the unsteady rolling of the plane brings back Tony's airsickness.

"I feel all rubbery . . ." says Tony.

"Just don't think about it," says Ed, as he feeds Tony ice and rubs the back of his neck.

With the plane on autopilot, Ed gives Tony oxygen, but it doesn't help; Tony gets sick twice, and they must make an unscheduled, but much needed pit stop in Chattanooga, then again in Kingsport, Tennessee.

Determined not to be beaten by bad weather and his own airsickness, Tony takes to the skies again to do battle with the elements. Tony makes it through the worst of the weather and heads north, toward Massachusetts.

Exhausted and sick to his stomach, Tony sees the end in sight. He has successfully navigated his way to Massachusetts, and he sets down to be greeted by a group of reporters even larger than the groups he left behind—but most importantly, his parents and his sister Alaina are there to welcome him.

Tony has done it! He has broken the record, and is the youngest pilot in the world to fly across the United States!

Over the next few days, Tony is issued a citation from the Massachusetts Senate for his feat, as well as a citation from the National Aeronautic Association. Down in Washington, Tony is honored by a presentation at the National Air and Space Museum, in front of the *Spirit of St. Louis*—Charles Lindbergh's famous plane, which flew the first transatlantic flight.

After spending Easter with his grandparents, Tony flies back to California, in three calm, uneventful days. His round trip total is six thousand miles!

Not one to be bested, Christopher Lee Marshall, the boy whose record Tony broke, has since flown across the Atlantic Ocean, re-creating Lindbergh's famous flight. In addition to that, eleven year-old Jennifer Hudgens flew a Cessna 181 from southern Florida to northern Alaska—4,100 miles—making her the youngest girl ever to pilot a plane across the country—and proving that girls are every bit as able as boys.

Is Tony going to go for any more records—perhaps even take on Christopher Marshall's transatlantic flight?

"I don't know," says Tony. "Actually, I want to fly around the world," he says with a smile. Perhaps he's just kidding, or perhaps he means it, but one thing is certain, Tony can certainly do it if he sets his mind to it.

And if not, well, he'll settle down and go back to his little league team, and Nintendo, and skateboarding. After all there's more to life than being a pilot—being a brain surgeon, for instance—which is what Tony *really* wants to be when he grows up!

UPDATE: FRIENDSHIP FLIGHT '89

Tony wasn't kidding.

Just a year after his record-breaking cross-country flight, Tony set off on "Friendship Flight '89"—Tony's dream flight around the world, which was far more daring, and far more celebrated, than any of his earlier flights.

It began on June 5, 1989. Tony, having just turned eleven, took off from John Wayne Airport with two other planes by his side. Flying in Tony's plane were his parents and sister, an observer from the National Aeronautic Association, and Tony's Soviet pen pal, Roman Tcheremynkh. Flying in the chase planes were Soviet and American journalists, as well as a documentary film crew.

The trip was to take forty-seven days, and took Tony through Canada, Iceland, Norway, Sweden, Finland, and the Soviet Union. Tony flew a grueling three hours each day, with just a few days of rest throughout the 21,567-mile trip.

The goal of the flight was to bring a message of

peace to the Soviet people—a "Friendship Scroll," filled with a thousand feet of signatures from American children. Tony presented the scroll to Soviet leader Mikhail Gorbachev, and in return, Tony was presented with a similar scroll signed by Soviet children.

After presenting the scroll in Moscow, and meeting with countless Soviet kids, Tony set off on the most difficult part of his journey—a seven-thousand-mile crossing of the Soviet Union, which made Tony the first private pilot ever to cross the breadth of the Soviet Union. At times, he flew over areas so remote and desolate that he was far beyond the reach of radar—and some parts of the trip forced Tony to negotiate his way through towering mountain ranges, testing his ability in the most dangerous of situations.

In Alaska, after Tony had made it across the Soviet Union and just days short of the flight's completion, disaster struck. Having made it this far, Tony and company decided to take a little break from the Friendship Flight and take a three-day fishing trip. Since the side trip wasn't part of the flight, Tony's dad piloted the plane—but the gravel airstrip in the tiny Eskimo village of Golovin was a disaster waiting to happen. He lost control of the plane, and the aircraft plummeted down a fifty-foot embankment, into a swamp. One of the wings caught fire on impact, and the plane was virtually destroyed.

It was a disaster—but it was also a miracle, because no one was injured.

Undaunted, Tony took to the air again, in a borrowed plane, and landed in John Wayne Airport, five days later, to the sight of cheering crowds.

Now that they're all back home, the Aliengenas are determined that their lives will once again return to normal. As for Tony, well, when asked what's in store for him next, he laughed and said, "Maybe I'll fly pole-to-pole." Of course, he was only joking, but with Tony, you never really know . . .

Just for Fun . . .

Everyone knows that garlic smells really good when it's in food, but when it's on someone's breath, they might as well be breathing radiation! But how about using garlic on your hands and face? That's right, garlic soap.

Damon Kheir-Eldin's first experience with garlic came when he was eight years old. He seemed to get more than his fair share of colds and flu, so his third-grade teacher suggested that he either take garlic tablets or eat garlic cloves.

Although there is no medical support for this, some people feel that garlic may help the body's immune system fight germs. If nothing else, the garlic on Damon's breath would keep sick people away!

Damon was trying to come up with an idea for his seventh-grade science fair project for Schaghti-coke Middle School, in New Milford, Connecticut. He remembered that his mother was always telling him to wash his hands and came up with the idea of making a stronger soap. While working on this he made an interesting discovery. Damon found that garlic combined with soap kills more germs than soap alone!

His liquid soap is made up of salad oil, water, baking soda, melted household soap, and garlic juice extracted from garlic cloves.

A nurse at the science fair was impressed with Damon's discovery and brought the soap to the local hospital, where its future will be determined.

That was last year. This year, Damon did more garlic research—he developed a natural garlic pesticide that won him second place in the Connecticut state science fair!

Damon could be on to something very big here. Something very smelly, but very big!

Chrissie McKenney:
A Voice in the Silence

There's probably a lot of kids who could do what eleven-year-old Chrissie McKenney does, but the point is that other kids don't. It takes a great amount of caring for a kid to want to spend time working with the deaf—Chrissie's kind of caring. Chrissie is the youngest volunteer at the Mississippi School for the Deaf, and has mastered the skill of two-handed signing. She has a lot to say about her work. . . .

I was nine when I started. I've been doing it for two years. It all started at my church—you see, we have this "expressive worship" thing at the church, where you sign along with some of the songs. That's how I got interested in sign language.

One day we were driving past the school for the deaf, and I asked my mom if we could stop in and see if there was anything I could help with. When we went in, they told us that they normally don't let children under sixteen volunteer, but if my mom came with me, they said they'd make an exception.

I work with about thirteen girls who are a little bit younger than me. I volunteer on Thursday afternoons, and help them prepare for what they're doing in the evening. When there's time left over, I read to them, using sign language.

Sign language isn't too hard—it's about the same as learning the basics of a foreign language. My mom says signing is a lot easier for kids because kids catch on to things quicker than adults. It was really easy for me, but Mom had a little more trouble than I did. Besides English, sign language is the only other language I know. I took a Spanish class when I was really little, but I don't remember anything.

Signing works like this: you make motions that are similar to what the word means. Not all words have signs. Some you have to spell by using signed letters. I know American Sign Language, but signing is different in different countries.

I'm really glad I volunteer, because it's a rewarding experience. I love it when I come in and the kids all run to me and hug me—each one wants me to be with them at the same time! I have some friends at school who want to volunteer too. I taught them sign language. Well . . . they *say* they want to volunteer, but they haven't yet.

I think lots of people are afraid of working with the deaf. They don't remember that deaf people are exactly the same as everybody else—it's just that they can't hear. If a person who could was in a room with fifty deaf people, the hearing person would be the one with the handicap.

I'm gonna continue volunteering. Sure, I could be out playing soccer or baseball or basketball, or doing other stuff I like, but I can do that other times. Helping the deaf doesn't take all my time.

When I grow up, I want to do volunteer work with the deaf, and have a career in something else. I might like to be a comedian, because I like making people laugh. It makes me feel good when people laugh and are happy.

Zebulon Roche: Master of the Mountain

Fifteen-year-old Zebulon Roche skis down the impossibly steep slope, in perfect control. He weaves around the jagged rocks that jut out of the French alpine peak, following the paths of snow.

Ahead of him is a sheer five-hundred foot cliff. There is no way, at the speed Zebulon is skiing, that he can avoid falling off the cliff. He has no intention of stopping. He leans forward, picks up speed, rockets off the mountain, and flies into the air, hundreds of feet above the jagged rock. As he begins that terrible fall, he pulls a cord on his backpack. A parachute flies out of his pack, and he goes sailing down to a soft landing.

It's called parapetting, and it's one of the many adventurous things Zebulon Roche does each day. Zebulon, at fifteen, is one of the world's most accomplished mountain climbers.

Zebulon is from a mountainous area of France. When his father, a ski instructor and mountain guide, saw that Zebulon, at age five, was interested in rock climbing, he was pleased. Rock climbing is a sport similar to mountain climbing; however, rock climbers use their hands and feet instead of ropes.

Zebulon ran into problems right away. First of all, there was no climbing equipment small enough for a five-year-old. He couldn't even hold the ice pick. As Zebulon grew up, his family had special equipment made for him, from his ice pick to his boots. Even when he began parapetting at age twelve things didn't quite work the way they should have. The first time Zebulon parapetted off of a mountain, his chute was so large and he was so light that the air lifted him up, and he blew away, over the mountain. A smaller chute solved that problem!

For Zebulon Roche, adventure is a way of life. He graduated from rock climbing to mountain climbing when he was eleven, with a spectacular climb: He scaled the highest peak in the Alps— Mont Blanc, rising 15,781 feet! The next year, he took on the sheer face of El Capitan in Yosemite National Park. Then only a few weeks later, he climbed 3,600 feet straight up the rock wall of "Super-Crack" in Utah. As if this weren't enough, he followed these feats with a 1,250-mile cross-country ski trip over the Alps, with his father.

That ski trip won him the distinction of being named French Young Adventurer of the year.

The young adventurer has also been in a film he and his father made about their adventures—but in spite of all his fame, Zebulon considers himself just a regular kind of guy, who likes to have fun climbing, skiing, and parapetting in the winter, then canoeing and kayaking in the summer.

Like everyone else, Zebulon has a dream, but his is a little higher than most people's—twenty-nine thousand feet higher! You see, Zebulon dreams of climbing Mount Everest, the world's highest mountain, which looms over five miles high.

Naturally, once he climbs up, he has no intention of climbing down. Why should he? He plans to jump off the top, and parachute the many miles back to the mountain's base!

Janet Evans: Dangerous When Wet

When Janet Evans was given her first swimming lesson at age one, everyone could see how quickly she took to the water—but no one could have guessed that just sixteen years later she would be one of the most celebrated athletes of the 1988 Summer Olympics!

Janet's introduction to the water was more out of convenience than out of design. Her mom had brought her older brothers to a swimming lesson, and Janet, being a very active baby, simply couldn't sit still with her mother in the stands. Finally her mom asked if the instructors could take Janet and give her lessons as well. They agreed, and the rest is history!

By age three, Janet had mastered the crawl and had learned the breast stroke and the butterfly stroke. At age ten, Janet set a national record for children ten and under in the 200-meter freestyle (crawl) event—and her record still stands today.

Through all of this, Janet had to overcome an obstacle that could have discouraged her from pursuing her sport: Janet was always small for her age. In swimming, where races are won by hundredths of a second, tall swimmers have an advantage; they use fewer strokes to cross the pool.

At meets, referees would take one look at Janet's height, and try to force her to swim with younger kids. "You belong with the ten-year-olds," they would tell Janet when she was twelve. She would argue, and would finally be allowed to swim with girls her age. Other girls would take one look at her and snicker—as if it were a joke that they had to race against one so small. What Janet lacked in size, however, she made up for in skill, and none of her opponents laughed when she hit the touch-pad first, winning the race, and blowing everyone else's times out of the water!

Being a world-class swimmer is more than just swimming races and winning. Behind every victory are hours of grueling workouts. At age thirteen, Janet began training for the Olympics, working out eleven times a week. Her entire schedule, and even her family's schedule, revolves around her workouts.

Janet's morning workouts begin at five A.M., and last until seven. After school she weight-trains for half an hour before returning to the pool for her afternoon workout. She swims fifteen thousand meters each day, and at night is in bed by eight-thirty.

With all that exercise, Janet needs to eat a lot just to keep up her energy. She eats four meals a day, and is constantly snacking—but it's all burned off in her workouts.

You might think that her grades and social life would suffer because of her rigid swimming schedule—but you'd be wrong. Janet isn't a straight-A student, but she maintains an A-minus average. As for her social life, well, she dates the student body president, and just three months before the Olympics she was crowned princess of the junior prom.

About a year before the Olympics, Janet's hard work began to pay off. When Janet was sixteen, she shattered the three oldest records in swimming—records that had stood for almost ten years. Little Janet Evans, standing only five feet, five and a half inches tall, became the world's fastest swimmer in the 400-meter, 800-meter, and 1,500-meter free-style events.

Janet's speed has amazed a great many people. One man did an experiment that analyzed the contents of Janet's exhaled air by having her swim and breathe out into a tube connected to a weather balloon. He concluded that Janet uses less oxygen and less energy to swim than any of the thousand other swimmers he had tested. In short, Janet Evans is the most efficient human swimming machine in the world—male or female.

* * *

Janet trained her last few weeks in Hawaii, then finally it was time to leave for Seoul, South Korea. Janet brought her schoolwork along with her to the Olympics.

Her first race was the 400-meter I.M.—that is, individual medley—a grueling race in which the swimmer starts off with butterfly, switches to backstroke, then breast stroke, and finishes off the last one hundred meters swimming freestyle. It has never been Janet's strongest event.

At that point in the Olympic games, not a single gold medal had yet gone to U.S. athletes. Matt Biondi wanted to tie Mark Spitz's record of seven gold medals, but when Matt lost his first race, that dream was left for another Olympiad.

With the eyes of the world on her, Janet began her race at the sound of the gun.

Janet swam the butterfly leg of her I.M. After the first hundred yards of the race, however, she was in fourth place. Butterfly is Janet's weakest stroke, and she had to make up for lost time if she were to take any medal at all. She took the lead during the backstroke and held it for the entire race, taking America's first gold medal, and beating Romania's Noemi Lung by more than a body length. She set a new American record of 4 minutes, 37.76 seconds.

There were two more events for Janet—the 400 and 800 freestyle. Having set the world records in both events, she made winning both gold medals look easy, and finished off the Olympics with a remarkable three out of three gold medals.

What makes Janet Evans so fast? Surely her determination and hard training play an important part, but her attitude helps as well. From the time Janet was young, her parents were always more concerned with her having fun than her coming home with a medal. This positive attitude shines through in everything she does. You only have to look at Janet to see she's having the time of her life when she swims, for when she's not cutting through the water at superhuman speed, Janet can always be found with a smile on her face.

"I'm smiling," said Janet after one of her Olympic events, "because I'm having fun. That's what this is all about: having fun!"

Just for Fun . . .

A very special congratulations to eight-year-old Robert Scruton of Montpelier, Vermont. Robert didn't parachute off a mountain, or save his mother from the jaws of an angry crocodile, but he did win a very noble and sought-after award in Montpelier. Robert was the proud winner of the thirteenth annual National Rotten Sneaker Contest.

Yes, that's right, Robert was rewarded for having the world's grungiest sneakers!

So, hats (and shoes) off to Robert Scruton. Maybe he should wash his shoes in garlic soap. Now that would *really* be gross!

Ray Bateman:
The Medicine Man

A few years from now, thousands of people may owe their lives to the work of fifteen-year-old Ray Bateman, but they'll probably never know it. When you work in the medical research field, there really isn't that much glory—except the satisfaction of knowing you've taken mankind one step closer to conquering disease.

Ray has now spent several years working under his friend Dr. Glen Tisman, and the amazing results they have achieved in cancer research have been enough to make the entire medical community stand up and take notice of this fifteen-year-old whiz kid.

Ray already sounds a bit like a doctor himself when he explains the complicated nature of his work, and how it all began. . . .

I always knew I was pretty good with mechanical things. When I was four, my mom's vacuum cleaner broke down. I took it apart and fixed it. When I was just a few years older, I would build lots of things from kits that were meant for adults. When I was nine, I built a TV from a kit and I even added some features that weren't included in the kit—like picture filtration, and some other things.

I've known Dr. Tisman since I was pretty young, because his son and I were friends. One time he got a big stereo system that needed to be assembled, and he couldn't do it, so he asked me. The thing took thirty hours to assemble, but I did it.

Sometime after that, he got a new machine in at his lab; a high-performance liquid chromatography machine, or HPLC for short. The manual was a thousand pages long, and the whole machine seemed pretty complicated, so he handed me the manual to see if I could make heads or tails out of it. He figured if I could put together that stereo, I could figure out this machine.

Well, basically, I didn't read the manual—I never read manuals, I just sort of browse through them and figure out what to do as I go along. I guess it just seemed pretty self-explanatory to me. Anyway, I figured out how the HPLC worked, and showed Dr. Tisman and the lab technicians who were going to be using the equipment. From there, I sort of just fell into doing research with him.

We're researching treatments for cancer, and the HPLC is an important device in our research. Basically, the machine measures the amount of a substance in a sample of blood, by showing on a graph how much ultraviolet light is absorbed by the sample. Once you know what a compound looks like when it appears on the graph, you can read the graph and know what's in the blood sample. I use it to test the concentration of certain drugs in people's blood after Dr. Tisman has given his patients the drug. By looking at the graph, I can tell how much of the drug remains in the blood and what the drug is being converted to in the body.

This is called chromatography. You might remember doing stuff in school called paper chromatography, where you take ink, or something, and put it on paper, and separate the ink into its separate colors. Basically the HPLC performs a very complicated version of that.

It's not an easy process—it's not like you can just stick something in the machine and it tells you how much of each substance is in the blood. You have to separate out the different compounds first, and you have to know exactly what you're looking for on the graph.

What we're looking for is the drug 5-FUDR, which is what Dr. Tisman has been giving his patients. We hope 5-FUDR will become a very important medicine for cancer patients. You see, back in the 1940s and '50s, there was this cancer drug called 5-FU (or 5-fluorouracil), but it wasn't very effective. About two years ago, however, it was found that when this drug was given with a vitamin derivative called leucovorin (derived from calcium B vitamins), the drug actually worked much better. Both Dr. Tisman and I believe that our drug,

5-FUDR (fluorodeoxyuridine) when given with the vitamin, will work even better still. It took up to five different steps for the body to convert the original drug, 5-FU, to its active state—the state it has to be in to fight cancer—but our drug only requires one step, so it goes to work much faster.

Once it's in its active state, it stops the body's production of DNA. If DNA can't be made, then the cancer can't grow.

Also, we're testing different doses. They used to just trickle the drug in very small amounts to exactly where in the body it was needed, but we're giving high doses intravenously. We've tried this on colon cancer, breast cancer, lung cancer, and cancer of the pancreas, and it seems to be working quite well.

What's good about this medication is that it's not going to take years and years to be approved. It's already approved, because it's just a combination of drugs that have been around for a long time—it's just that they haven't really been researched very much. It's the same way with lots of drugs, because so many drugs are invented, but few of them really get researched as much as they could be.

The work that I do mainly consists of reading charts and graphs, performing the lab work on the blood, background research, figuring out how to work new equipment, repairing old equipment, figuring out ways of separating compounds from our blood samples, and in general just coming up with better ways of doing things. I don't do any work directly with Dr. Tisman's patients, however, I do read the results of tests, and sometimes make recommendations to Dr. Tisman.

Some adults find it hard to believe that I'm actually doing the work I'm doing—but once they see I know what I'm talking about, they believe it.

Last year I even got the chance to go with Dr. Tisman to a meeting of the American Federation for Clinical Research, to give a presentation on the research we've been doing. It was really exciting for me. I was doing the presentation completely on my own—I made up all the slides on my computer and organized the whole thing. It was sort of nerve-racking to be up there in front of all those experts in medical research. I guess it wouldn't be so bad if you kind of didn't think about the five or six television cameras in the background.

I enjoy the work I do with Dr. Tisman, because it's challenging. A lot more challenging than school, that's for sure. I get bored with school pretty easily. My favorite subjects in school are math and science. I also feel English is important. I take French, but I don't like it very much, and I'm not a big fan of P.E.—although I do like sports, mainly water sports like waterskiing and sailing. I like to ski also.

Next year I'm going to a private school, and I'll only be home on weekends, so I won't have as much time to work on my research. During the school year it's always hard to do lab work. Usually I would set up the tests, the lab technicians would do the rest of the work, and I would analyze the results. I mean, it would be impossible to do everything *and* go to school for seven hours a day. During the summer, though, I have more time, and I spend about ten hours a day doing research. I take the weekends off, because I don't have any way to get to the lab on my own, and besides, I need to have some other life, right?

I spend all that time doing research, though, because I enjoy what I'm doing, and that's important. I think if you have an interest and you enjoy doing something specific, then no matter how crazy people may think you are, you should do it. Of course, that only goes so far, but if you're really interested in something, then research it as much as you can, and go do it.

As for me, I plan on going into medicine— applied research, where I not only sit and run tests and experiments, but get to work with patients as well.

Right now I'm working on some new things with Dr. Tisman, and we'll be going again to speak about it to the American Federation for Clinical Research. We're working on a test to measure a certain type of vitamin B-12 deficiency. The old test involves taking bone marrow from a patient for four days, and the results are often bizarre and incorrect. Now we're working on a way of doing it more accurately in one day.

After, all, that's my specialty: coming up with new and better ways of doing things!

Just for Fun . . .

What would it take to get you to give up watching TV? Would you do it on a dare? How about a double dare? How about for five hundred bucks?

One day eleven-year-old Betsy Clarke made a $500 bet with her parents that she could give up watching television for a whole year!

"What?" I hear you cry. "Give up TV? I would just as soon give up breathing, eating, and sleeping!"

Nowadays it seems hard to believe, but the human race survived thousands of years without the benefits of MTV, network primetime, or even Saturday morning cartoons. Amazing but true.

One year later, Betsy's parents lost their bet, and happily handed $500 to their daughter, who had managed to remain TV-free for 365 days!

It just goes to prove that there can be more to life than reruns of *The Brady Bunch*.

Walking on Water

It is September 22. The summer is over in Three Rivers, Michigan, and Clear Lake is cooling down for the winter. In the middle of the lake, a three-year-old girl in a blue and gold wet suit clings onto a boom bar jutting out from a speedboat. The boat accelerates, and beneath her, the cold lake rushes past at almost thirty miles per hour.

To most three-year-olds this could be a scene from a nightmare, but not to Chrystal Booko, who at six months old was doing underwater flips in swimming class. Gripping tightly onto the boom, Chrystal digs her heels into the water, and the water supports her, tickling and massaging the soles of her feet as she skims across the surface. The trip lasts for only a quarter of a mile, but it's enough to make Chrystal the youngest barefoot water-skier in the world.

* * *

That was over a year ago. Now, at age four, Chrystal is an old pro at barefoot waterskiing, just like her parents.

Chrystal lives on the shore of Clear Lake, in Michigan, and her parents, Dave and Cathy, are waterskiing enthusiasts. "We never really pushed her into doing this," they point out. "She wanted to do it herself."

"It began last summer," says Chrystal's mom. "She was watching her dad barefoot waterskiing, and she kept asking if she could try it too. We told her, 'well, maybe when you're a little older.' She could already water-ski, but we didn't know if she was ready to barefoot."

With the encouragement of skiing trainer Mike Seiple, the Bookos let their daughter ski her way into the record books.

Although too young for official competitions, Chrystal has still made quite a name for herself, and has five corporate sponsors, who provide her with skis, wet suits and everything she needs to keep her riding above water.

Barefoot waterskiing is not as easy as it looks, and Chrystal has had some bad spills. The worst one happened on Lake Osborne, in Florida. Chrystal was barefooting side by side with her father when all of a sudden the wake of another boat slammed into Chrystal's feet, and made her lose her balance. She sprawled for thirty yards on her belly, before falling face down into the cold lake.

"I don't want to barefoot anymore," she had told her father, with tears in her eyes, moments after they took her onto the speedboat, but ten minutes later she had forgotten all about it, and was already talking about barefooting on one foot—the next trick she wanted to learn.

Now Chrystal has mastered one-foot, and is hoping to learn the "back toe-up." That's when a skier starts underwater and is pulled up to a standing position with the rope attached to his or her toe. It's something her father has only just learned.

Even though there is no competition category for barefoot water-skiers under the age of twelve, Chrystal is hoping for some competition soon—because her two-year-old brother, Jordan, has been waterskiing since he was one. He hasn't tried barefooting yet, but when he does, Crystal had better watch out.

Rockin' Ricky Rocko

Quick-thinking, fast-talking Sam Rogoway, alias Ricky Rocko, knows a lot about rock music. You could say he's become one of the foremost authorities, because at nine years old, Rockin' Ricky Rocko is the world's youngest disc jockey.

Of course, Ricky's the first to tell you, being a DJ is not easy. . . .

I've been around radio stations all my life, because my dad used to be a disc jockey. When I was three years old I got a mini DJ set, and for years I practiced on it all the time—I wouldn't even leave it to go to dinner.

My dad was working at a small station in Vancouver, Canada. One day we were just fooling around, pretending that I was a disc jockey. We recorded it so we could keep a tape to listen to in the car. Well, the general manager walked in when we were doing this, and he flipped over it, thinking it would be a great gimmick to have the world's youngest DJ on his station. That was about a year and a half ago. I was eight.

I had to decide; do I use my real name on the air, or do I make up a name that sounds more like the name of a DJ? I was thinking about it, and then it came to me out of the blue: Little Ricky Rocko! I started to use the name on the air, and it felt kind of funny, because when people started calling me Ricky, I forgot they were talking to me, and didn't answer. I'm used to it now though. It's just like having two names.

Anyway, I didn't really like the format of that station—they played all oldies, and a lot of songs I didn't know. I like more modern rock—groups like INXS—and rap too, like Run D.M.C., so I switched to Z100, which is a big rock station up here in Portland. Now I'm on the air every Friday for *The Little Ricky Rocko Request Hour*, where people call in and request songs. Then on Saturdays, I have a five-minute rock report that gives all the rock news. It's fun!

When I first started at Z100 I was real scared, and you could tell that I was reading my lines, staring at the paper in front of me. It took a year to get really good at it, because I wasn't the greatest speaker, but now I've really improved. Now, I don't need to read from a paper; it's all me. I can introduce a song smoothly; I'll say something like, "Right now it's INXS, 'A New Sensation.' Yeah, I saw these guys in town and they were hot—right now they're hot on your stereo on Z100."

I can do everything pretty well now, but I made a lot of mistakes at first. Whenever I made a mistake, though, one of the other DJs would cover for me, and make it funny. Actually there's lots of things that can go wrong, and you have to make the bad things sound hilarious, to keep your listeners from switching stations. For instance, let's say I'm playing a record and it starts to skip over and over again. I'll have to turn on the mike and cover up. Sometimes DJs don't listen to the song playing while they're in the booth. They just turn down the volume, to plan what they're gonna do next. If they're not careful, the song might end and the station will be sending out dead air. That's the worst thing that can happen. Also, DJs might forget to turn off the mike once the song starts and the listeners can hear them talking over the song when they're not supposed to.

I remember one time I almost choked in the radio station during a song—not choked as in "froze up," but choked as in *really choked*—I couldn't breathe. When I got back on the air I was really frightened, I could barely talk, and I was afraid it would be my last day there ... but once I got on the air, I was okay. So you see, being a DJ might be a lot of fun, but it's really hard. You can't make mistakes.

Now I'm a lot better than when I started, and I've gotten to know the other DJs. We're like best friends. It's real fun working with *The Morning Zoo*, which is the morning show on Z100. There's four disc jockeys: two main ones, then Officer

Tony—he's our traffic man—and then our news lady. I'm just a special edition. *The Morning Zoo* has the funniest people on Z100.

Being funny is important. The most important thing about being a DJ is having a good personality; you have to be real quick, exciting, and jumpy. You can never be down. You have to work your audience on the air, like if you have a contest you have to really get them excited. No matter how you're feeling, you have to have lots of energy, and be happy.

In addition to music, and talking on the air, we have to put on commercials. All our commercials are on carts. A cart is sort of like a cassette tape, but a little bit bigger. You shove one into the cart machine, push a button, and it plays the commercial. Actually, lots of music is on cart too. It makes things easier—carts can't skip like records. Right now the station is just getting into CDs, so pretty soon, all our music will be on CD, and we'll even get CD commercials!

Being a DJ doesn't really affect my schoolwork, but it does change some things. I get mostly A's with a few B's in school. The fact that I have to miss Friday mornings doesn't really hurt my grades, and the principal thinks it's a good education for me—it's getting me ready for the big time. Sometimes, though, the kids are a problem.

The fifth graders hate me. I'm in third grade and I think the fifth graders are jealous. They even pick on my best friend because of it. I don't even know most of them, but they still pick on me.

But my friends like the fact that I'm a DJ. Sometimes I can even get concert tickets for them, or introduce them to rock stars backstage. I haven't met that many, but I've met a few—Tiffany, Belinda Carlisle, Bruce Hornsby, New Shoes, Vanessa Williams, and the Fat Boys.

My family, of course, really likes what I'm doing, my dad having been a DJ and all. Everyone gets involved. My dad's my manager, and brings me to the station. My mom does my hair, and picks out my clothes and stuff. I have a little brother who's seven, and he wants to be in the radio business too!

My dad and I have lots of fun. Like there was a time when my dad had a show on a rival station— KKSN—at the same time my show was on. It was like a fight between father and son over who was the best DJ, and so he would call up our station and do all of these pranks, so we would call up their station, and pull pranks on them! After the show my dad would pick me up, and we would both listen to our tapes to hear each other's show.

Things are going great now—I've even been on a few TV shows. I've been on *The Late Show*, *Hour Magazine*, *PM Magazine*, and a whole bunch more. I used to have a Rockin' Report I did for a local TV station, but it didn't work out. Someday, though, I'd like to have my own show.

I think I was really lucky to be able to get work as a DJ. I had connections, and I was in the right place at the right time. Now, there's lots of people asking for jobs, and they get turned away.

But now that I'm in, I want to stay in. When I grow up, I still want to be a DJ. Well, that or a basketball player!

Say Cheese!

The first thing that you notice about Milla Jovovich are her eyes. She'll capture you with a bright blue stare, and you'll know right away that this beautiful twelve-year-old girl was born to be a model.

Milla's story began seven years ago. Her mom was a Soviet actress. The family could have stayed in the Soviet Union, but Milla's father, a medical administrator, felt there would be more opportunities in America, so, after much paperwork, the family blazed a trail to Beverly Hills.

As Milla got older, it became clear how incredibly photogenic she was—that is, how well she photographed. Since last year, she's been on the cover of thirteen magazines, including *Seventeen* and *Mademoiselle*.

Recently, Milla has been in two films, *Two Moon Junction*, and *Night Train to Kathmandu*, and she

says she'll keep on modeling until she's as hot as
Brooke Shields!

Roll Over, Beethoven

If you've ever taken up a musical instrument, the first thing you learn is that playing is not as easy as it looks. To play any instrument well takes years of practice, and hours of patience. But once you put in all that time, you may become a virtuoso—like Tian Ying, or Ignat Solzhenitsyn. Or, you may become a composer like Dalit Paz Warshaw.

Dalit, now twelve years old, is the youngest of the three. She began playing piano at the age of three, and found that she had a talent for making up tunes. Dalit's mom taught her how to write down her made-up music in correct musical notation. As she grew, Dalit honed her skills, and by age nine she was composing music for entire orchestras! Her first orchestral piece is called "In the Beginning," and has been performed by orchestras around the nation.

* * *

Tian Ying was a child prodigy in mainland China. His parents, both of whom were involved in music, saw the boy's talent and enrolled him in the Shanghai Conservatory of Music at a very young age, and by the time he was eleven, Tian was playing piano with the Shanghai Symphony.

At age fourteen, Tian decided to broaden his horizons, and left home to study in America. His parents gave him their blessing, and he set off alone, to study at the New England Conservatory of Music, where he is today.

Now Tian collects piano competition awards like most kids collect baseball cards! Tian feels coming to study in America was the right move for him, and he hasn't been back to China since.

Ignat Solzhenitsyn has the most interesting background of all. His father is Aleksandr Solzhenitsyn, the legendary Nobel Prize winning author, famous for his books about the repression of people in the Soviet Union. Solzhenitsyn and his family were exiled from the Soviet Union eighteen months after Ignat was born.

Being the son of one of the most famous men of this century is not an easy thing, but at the age of four, Ignat began to show an interest in music—an interest which would eventually make a name for him, separate and apart from his father's fame. His family had just moved into a furnished house, and Ignat discovered a piano in one of the rooms. He immediately took to the instrument and began formal instruction at age nine. At first his playing was awful, as any beginner's is, but time, practice, and determination turned those sounds into wonderful music.

Ignat is now sixteen. He has studied in London for two years, has played over forty well-received concerts, and was featured as an up-and-coming artist in *People* magazine.

"A while back," he says, "people may have come to see me play because of my name, but now they come because they like what they hear."

Just for Fun . . .

There are three letters that can bring fear into the hearts of high school students. Those letters are *S-A-T*.

If you ever feel like the world's out to get you, and there's nothing you can ever do to improve your school grades, you might think of Chris LaFortuna.

Chris, a high school student in High Point, North Carolina, decided it was time to improve his attitude toward school. Perhaps with an improved attitude, he thought, he might do a little better.

With his new attitude, Chris managed to get a *perfect score* on his verbal SAT!

C'mon, Chris, can't you do better than that?!

Jeff Wood

Lots of kids spend hours on end talking on the phone, but few do it for the same reasons Jeff Wood does. When other kids talk on the phone, they may be talking about school, or what they want to see at the movies. When Jeff talks on the phone, he might be saving somebody's life. . . .

I man the phone lines at Talkline on Wednesday from three to six, and I'm always ready to sub for somebody, in case they can't show up. Kidsline and Talkline are for kids who have some sort of problem, and need to speak to someone. Kids call in, and we help them with problems. You'd be surprised what kinds of problems come up. We get latchkey kids who have trouble making dinner, or are fighting with their little brother—that's the easy stuff—but we also get kids calling in telling us that they're being abused, and sometimes teens call in and tell us they're about to commit suicide. When it's a really bad problem, we try to keep them on the line as long as possible, and we have "crisis intervention"—that is, we trace the call, and send the police over to wherever the kid is calling from.

I'm what you call a *mental health paraprofessional*—I volunteer my time to answer calls and help kids with their problems.

I first got involved with Talkline when I was fifteen, during my sophomore year of high school. I was doing a speech on latchkey kids, and I knew Talkline dealt with them a lot, so I called and they gave me lots of information. I worked with them closely for my speech, and the more I worked with them, the more interested I got.

That summer I decided to go through the training to be a paraprofessional, and man the phone lines. You have to be sixteen to get into the program, but they made an exception for me because I really wanted to do it. It was fifty hard hours of training. We heard different people speaking about how to deal with problems kids might have, and we did a lot of role playing. The role playing was the hardest. We would pretend to be talking to kids with problems and try to solve the problems they came up with. The instructors played the parts of the kids. Role playing is really hard, but it gets you ready for working on the lines.

Pretty soon I found out that I was good at helping kids, and I got a lot of satisfaction out of it. I'm not a latchkey kid, but I can relate to them, and I know what it's like to be home and bored. I found that I worked real well with kids. My methods were a little bit unorthodox—when kids call, most volunteers simply try to find the kid on the line something constructive to do, and try to get them off the phone quickly. I wouldn't do that. My shift partner and I would tell jokes to the kids, and keep them on the lines longer than most would. We'd have them write to us, so we were more involved with them than other people. We're just really enthusiastic about it. It got to the point where the same kids would call every week just to talk to us! It felt great to be able to build up a rapport with kids. Normally kids won't tell you lots of things, but when you build up a rapport with them, they will. They might even tell you troubles that they're afraid to tell anyone else. For instance, there was this one little girl who would call each week because she was lonely, then after a while she told me that her mom was abusing her. Kids are comfortable talking to me because I'm close to them in age. I can really do a lot of good on the phone.

We're not allowed to call the kids. They don't even know our last names—that's one of the rules—but they can write to us, and we'll write back. That's how we started the Jeff and Andy Fan Club.

Andy (that's my shift partner) and I told kids to write in to the Jeff and Andy Fan Club, and pretty soon we were getting lots of letters. There are some kids that I haven't spoken to in over a year, but they still write!

We started a newsletter too, and got Judy Blume to contribute money so we could get the newsletter out to three hundred thousand kids. The newsletter was filled with things to do while you're bored. It had games, crossword puzzles, cartoons, and a whole lot of creative stuff.

Lots of scary stuff happens while you're on the lines. Once this little boy called and said he had run away from home, and took his father's shotgun. He said he needed protection. I talked to him for a while. "What are you going to do?" I asked, and he said, "Well I have twenty dollars." I said, "Do you think twenty dollars is going to get you very far?" He thought and said, "No."

So I suggested he stay home and try to work everything out with his parents. He listened!

The next week I get a call from the boy, and he tells me that everything's okay. He was getting an allowance and was much happier. It turns out that he had tried to call me every day that week until he finally got me to thank me. Things like that make me feel real good.

Once we had a rash of teenage suicides in the Chicago area. We were getting suicide call after suicide call, which was really abnormal for us. I've gotten suicide calls that have been really close. Sometimes they say things like, "Well, I'm okay now, but as soon as I hang up the phone, I'm gonna kill myself." We have to keep them on the line and just hope they stay on till the police get there.

The advice we give can never really backfire, because we give "self-discovery" advice. That is, we help kids help themselves. For instance, when a kid gets on the lines with a problem, we'll have them list all their alternatives, and have them pick the best one. They help themselves, we just direct them.

But sometimes, no matter what you do, things don't go the way you want them to. There was this girl who kept calling and telling us she was being abused by her mother. But the policeman I sent over knew the mother, and so nothing was done about it. The girl kept calling—she was doing worse and worse in school, she kept telling me all these horrible stories, and began to even make up lies—she wanted attention so badly, and there was nothing I could do. She wasn't getting the help she needed. The director of Talkline told me that I should tell her to stop calling, because she wasn't taking our advice or helping herself at all. When she called, I told her that I couldn't spend all this time talking to her anymore and she got real quiet and sad and teary. There was nothing I could do. I couldn't help her. I never found out what happened to her.

But then there are the times good things happen. There was this one sixteen-year-old girl who was getting pressure from her peers and from her parents. She wanted to kill herself, so I signaled my partner, and got a trace on the call. I built up a trust with the girl, and talked her problems through with her. Finally, while she was still on the phone, the police got to her house, and spoke to her. She called me back the next month to thank me and tell me everything was much better. Getting calls like that make me feel really good!

The Sharp Eye
of Denise Parker

Robin Hood may have some stiff competition. South Jordan, Utah, may be far away from Sherwood Forest, but that didn't stop fourteen-year-old Denise Parker from becoming one of the best archers in the world.

Denise had learned to shoot a bow and arrow four years ago, so that she and her parents could take hunting trips together. Three years later, at the age of thirteen, Denise won the gold medal at the Pan American Games. She is the youngest archer ever to win the gold in individual archery competition!

Success doesn't come easily though: Denise trains with her dad ten hours a week, and says it's her parent's love and support that have made her a great archer. In addition to her gold medal at the Pan American Games, she holds ten national Junior Girls records.

Denise was the youngest member of the 1988

U.S. Olympic Team, and although she didn't bring home the archery medals this time, she knows she'll have the chance again. She'll be only eighteen at the 1992 Olympics in Barcelona.

The Champ in Tramp

The world may appear upside-down to sixteen-year-old Terry Butler, but that's the way he wants it to be. You see, Terry is the top-ranked trampolinist in the United States.

It all began when Terry was eight. He was watching his older sister perform on a trampoline, and he said to himself, "I can do that," and set out to prove it. Eight years later, he can jump thirty feet into the air, and do a double back somersault with two twists—perhaps the hardest move on a trampoline.

The highest rank for a trampolinist is the "elite" rank, and most of the nation's fifty elite trampolinists are in their early twenties. Terry was ranked as an elite before his twelfth birthday.

Terry attributes his success in gymnastics to his natural ability, as well as to confidence and determination—after all, no matter what you're born with, says Terry, if you don't believe you can do something, you won't be able to do it!

Right now Terry is working on his diving skills so he can get a college scholarship—but trampoline is still foremost in his mind. Right now, although he's the top-rated trampolinist in the country, he's ranked eighth in the world, and Terry knows he can do better than that!

The Alley Cats

Two bowling lanes side by side. A seven-year-old boy and his mirror image approach the lanes, and with practiced skill release their balls. Each ball rumbles down the alley, smashing into the ten pins at the far end, bringing them all down. Two strikes, right beside one another.

If you saw it, you might shake your head and blink. "It's an optical illusion," you might say to yourself. "It's just one bowling lane, with a mirror right beside it."

But you'd be wrong.

It's seven-year-old Scott and Matthew Higa, the two bowlers of Colma, California, doing what they do best.

Scott and Matthew began their brilliant bowling careers four years ago. Their parents, Tom and Judy, are bowling enthusiasts, and the plastic bowling set they had bought the boys at age two just wasn't good enough anymore. At the age of three, the twins took to the real lanes, joining a pint-sized bowling league in their hometown. When they first started, they averaged about thirty points a game, but by the age of five—weighing only about five times as much as the bowling balls themselves— both Matthew and Scott had bowled hundred-point games, and were the stars of their league.

Back then, the boys had to bowl two-handed, bouncing the ball off their tummies to send it rolling down the lane, but at age six, they began using the standard one-arm delivery of their ten-pound balls. Now they are no longer the "bowling babies," as they had been called; they are talented young men, with averages close to 110, and over forty bowling trophies decorating their home—even more trophies than their parents have won!

The twins have become celebrities in their hometown of Colma, a suburb of San Francisco, and recently gained the support of close to one hundred sponsors for a special fund-raising bowling event, in which they raised much-needed money for Alzheimer's disease research.

What's next for these second-grade bowling stars? Well, to them knocking down the pins is easy. *Now* they have to figure out how to keep score by themselves!

American Brainstormers

Do you bump your head whenever you do the backstroke? How about a pair of rearview swimming goggles?

Does your baby sitter always bang her head while taking a bath? How about a rubber-baby-bathtub-bumper?

Can't decide whether to walk or roller-skate to school? How about transforming jogging shoes?

And are you tired of dropping the football every time it's passed to you? Well, what about a Velcro-covered football?

These are just some of the wild but ingenious inventions developed by kids across the nation for the Invent America competition. The Invent America awards are given out annually to kids from kindergarten through eighth grade, in every state, to honor bright ideas and creative solutions to all sorts of problems.

Believe it or not, kids can sometimes be better inventors than adults because kids don't have that "it can't be done" attitude. For a kid, anything is possible, and that's proved by some of the clever creations honored by Invent America.

The problems the award winners have tackled range from a solution to the world's energy problems, to a kid who just wanted an easy way of clipping his parrot's toenails.

Most inventions fall into several different categories. Some inventions are medical in nature. For instance, everyone knows that too much salt in one's diet can lead to high blood pressure. Well, eight-year-old Lisa Labadie came up with visible salt— salt that is dyed red, so you can see when you're using too much. A fifth grader by the name of Josh Jorde came up with a pulse-watcher, which lets the wearer know if his or her pulse is falling too low.

Some inventors took on solving the problems of the handicapped. For instance, did you ever notice how some obnoxious people take the handicapped parking space even though they're not handicapped? Well, Daniel Coudriet, a fourth grader, invented an alarm system that goes off if the driver does not insert a special handicap card into the meter. Other inventions for the handicapped range from braille labels on canned food to a smoke detector for the deaf.

Annoyances of everyday life were tackled by many inventors. Like when you're on an airplane and the bozo next to you falls asleep, letting his head fall right into you? Well, eleven-year-old Michael Oliveras of Brooklyn, New York, designed a headrest that keeps the bozo's head in place!

Or what about all those times when people are caught with their flies open? Well, Michael Bysiek came up with the Zipper Alarm, to warn of potential disaster. The only question is, which is more embarrassing: being caught with your fly open, or having your zipper alarm go off in a crowd?

Some inventors created handy household items, like nine-year-old Julie Gallo's mess-free disposable-sheet grossless flyswatter, or Michael Bysiek's other invention, the electric toilet paper dispenser!

If any of this sounds wild and crazy, just remember, some of the greatest ideas of all time weren't taken seriously at first. Look at Thomas Alva Edison, the inventor of the light bulb, motion pictures, sound recording, and countless other things that we take for granted today. At first no one took his "crackpot" ideas seriously.

Sometimes inventions and great ideas can come ahead of their time. Many of us know the story of Preston Tucker, who, almost forty years ago, designed a car with amazing new innovations, such as seat belts, and shatterproof glass. The automobile industry pushed him out of business, simply because his cars were too good for their time. More recently, just twelve years ago, a company began selling personal computers for $750, but nobody bought any, because the idea was simply three years too soon!

So if you dream of some invention, be it a new

musical instrument that's half trumpet, half trombone, or a car wash for horses, always remember that the most earth-shattering of inventions have often had the humblest of beginnings!

Here's a list of 1988's national award winning inventors, from first through eighth grade:

NAME: Lesage Wisniewski
GRADE: Kindergarten
HOMETOWN: Waldorf, Maryland
INVENTION: "Sur-footer," a device to help small children figure out which shoe goes on which foot.

NAME: Collin Hazen
GRADE: First
HOMETOWN: Fargo, North Dakota
INVENTION: "Puppy Finder," a dog collar that lights up at night to make your pet easier to find, and keeps it safe from traffic.

NAME: Lillian Ruth Lucas
GRADE: Second
HOMETOWN: Arlington, Massachusetts
INVENTION: "Puddle Detecting Cane," a cane that alerts blind people when they are about to step into a puddle.

NAME: Caitlin McCracken
GRADE: Third
HOMETOWN: Exeter, Rhode Island
INVENTION: "Orphan Kitten Feeder for Three," an animal feeder that feeds baby animals with no mother, and for use in animal hospitals.

NAME: Daniel Coudriet
GRADE: Fourth
HOMETOWN: Richmond, Virginia
INVENTION: "Handicap Helper," a system that prevents nonhandicapped people from using handicapped parking spaces.

NAME: Andy Hardaker
GRADE: Fifth
HOMETOWN: Jacksonville, Florida
INVENTION: "Underwater Jungle Gym," for fun and to improve swimming skills.

NAME: Matthew Ghormley
GRADE: Sixth
HOMETOWN: Oak Ridge, Tennessee
INVENTION: "Cello Stopper," which, when attached to a cello player's chair, stabilizes the instrument.

NAME: Cam Raines
GRADE: Seventh
HOMETOWN: Sandersville, Georgia
INVENTION: "Vein Detector," a device for heating

up a patient's arm, making it easier for the doctor to see the veins in order to take blood.

NAME: Randal Six
GRADE: Eighth
HOMETOWN: Worland, Wyoming
INVENTION: "Let the Sun Shine," an inexpensive
    solar heater.

Nine Steps to Your Own Invention

1. Speak to people and find out what problems they would like to see solved.
2. Of those problems select the most interesting.
3. Begin keeping a journal of ideas.
4. Do some research and find out if anyone else has tried to solve the problem.
5. Start thinking about solutions and writing them down in your journal.
6. Once you've found the best solution, create your invention.
7. Remember, just because it sounds good and looks good, doesn't mean that it works. Test your invention over and over again.
8. Think about how you might want to sell your invention. Who would need it? How can you let people know about it?
9. Plan a presentation to tell and show people what your invention does. Your presentation should be only about three minutes long.

If your invention is good enough, you may find yourself a winner of an Invent America award—or better yet—the inventor of the wonder gadget of tomorrow!

For more information about Invent America, write to:

INVENT AMERICA
The Patent Model Foundation
1331 Pennsylvania Ave., NW, Suite 903
Washington, D.C. 20004

Newsflash!

Things aren't always easy at Juan Cordova's school. It's in a rough neighborhood, where gangs rule the streets and sometimes even the schools. In that kind of neighborhood, there's nothing a fifth grader can do, is there?

Wrong!

When ten-year-old Juan saw that some of his friends were being picked on by neighborhood gang members from high school and junior high, Juan went to the police.

That might not sound like much, but remember, this was a neighborhood where even the adults were afraid to turn in the local hoods, because these gang members always got back at anyone who turned them in. Still, little Juan went right ahead, even though the gang threatened to beat him up if he told the police.

Because of what Juan did, other members of his community volunteered to help and get the bad kids off of the street. In the end many of the gang members were convicted of robbery and other crimes—all thanks to Juan Cordova, a boy who set an example not only for other kids, but for grown-ups as well.

David's Game

"... **O**kay, so the queen moves up and back, sideways and diagonal, and the knights move up two and over one, or over two and up one and they can jump too, right? Got it? Good. Now the pawns move forward and that's all they can do. Well, yeah, they capture diagonally ... except, of course, when they capture by en passant, which is sideways. Sort of. And then of course every once in a while a pawn becomes a queen, but they have to be really good pawn ..."

If this all sounds very confusing to you, imagine how it might sound to a six-year-old. Chess is definitely not like go-fish. There are lots of rules, and the game is filled with levels of strategy that make it one of the world's most fascinating board games.

Six-year-old David Peterson knows all about chess. He started playing at the age of five, and now, a year later, is ranked as the nation's best six-year-old chess player. David competed for his title at the National Junior High School Chess Championship—where more than 450 kids from thirty-six states competed. David won his age group with flying colors, proving something most chess players already know: The rules of chess aren't as complicated as they sound, and anyone could learn to play!

Michelle's Dream of
Peace

If you ever think that kids have no voice in what goes on in the world, you may want to think about Michelle Alexander. This twelve-year-old girl has done more for world peace than most people do in their entire lives. As Michelle will tell you, it all has to do with a vision of the future, and the determination to make a difference. Michelle has certainly made quite a difference—enough of a difference to be nominated for the first annual Reebok Human Rights Award!

Here's what Michelle has to say about world peace:

When I was in third grade my teacher assigned us to come up with inventions of the future. I didn't know what I was going to do—a friend of the family suggested a war game, but that idea really disturbed me. I definitely wouldn't want to play a war game.

I started thinking about the world. That night, I had this nightmare that the world was blown up, and I went in crying to my parents' room. "I want to grow up," I told them. "I don't want to die when I'm young."

They told me that if I felt that strongly about it, I should start promoting peace, and that's just what I did. I knew what I wanted to invent for class: a world peace game.

I came up with a board game called "Give Peace a Chance." The game works like this. You get one hundred and seventy national flags to choose from. Then you move around the board, and you gain tokens by being peaceful, and lose tokens by being warlike. There's lots of talking involved—negotiating and compromising with other nations. Sometimes it can get pretty realistic.

My teacher had put some of the best class projects at our local museum in Fresno, and the press came to do a story on them. My invention seemed to get lots of interest, and before I knew it, there were people who wanted to buy it, so we began making bunches of them.

That was back in third grade, and now I'm in seventh. It's amazing how the game has changed my life! It got so much publicity that the leaders of nations all around the world had heard of it—it has won awards, and was even on display at the United Nations. We've sold thousands of them all around the world.

Before long, I found myself as sort of a leader in a children's peace movement. Now I fly all around the world, at the invitation of world leaders, so that we can talk about peace, and play the game. I've played with the prime minister of Norway, President Rajiv Gandhi of India, and the vice president of the People's Republic of China, to name a few. I've been to one hundred and fifty-eight countries in the past few years!

I've even played with Andrey Gromyko, then president of the Soviet Union. We played in the Kremlin—I was really excited to play the game with him. I liked him, because he looked straight in my eyes when we talked. He made a joke—you see, in the board game, you move to the right, and he said, "No, in the Soviet Union, we move to the *left*!" I didn't get that until my mom explained it to me. I won't tell you who won the game. After all, it's the playing that matters, not who wins. Besides, telling who won wouldn't be diplomatic!

Afterward we had a talk about peace, and how the kids of my generation want to grow up without the fear of war.

Now, I feel like I've really become involved in the world peace movement. After Reagan and Gorbachev signed their weapons treaty, I sent a letter to Mr. Gorbachev, thanking him for helping to ensure that our world is a better place to live—for letting the world see that people of the Soviet Union are just like us, and everyone wants a world free of war.

We've been invited back to the Soviet Union, and

next time I'll be playing the game with Mr. Gorbachev.

I spend lots of time promoting peace in the Soviet Union now. I write a peace column for the *Novosti Press*, a Soviet newspaper.

I've also become a regular at the United Nations. It's gotten so that when I walk in, the guard says, "Hi Michelle," and doesn't check my bag or anything, because he trusts me.

I was once invited to this closed press conference at the UN, being conducted by the Soviet delegation for the World Press. I remember some guards came over and asked why I was there, and a man in the Soviet delegation stood up and said, "She is my guest, that is why she is here." I was introduced, and had a chance to talk with the press about the peace game. After the conference, I gave my letter for Mr. Gorbachev to the delegate, who assured me the letter would be hand-delivered to Mr. Gorbachev!

In addition to the peace game I've started the Peace Pal Club—an international pen pal club. When I travel around the world and speak to large groups of kids, I have them give me postcards with their addresses on them, and match them with pen pals in other countries. All kids like to receive mail and so I know kids will like doing it. It's already starting to work nicely.

Through all of this, I have to thank my parents for their love and support. This whole peace business has become a full-time job for my mom—you know, traveling around the world with me, and promoting the game, and peace and all that. The game is selling really well, and they've even translated it into Russian. We donate half the money we make from the game to peace organizations that deal directly with kids. I think it's the right thing to do.

I'm glad to be doing what I'm doing. I think it's important to learn about different cultures, and learn how to cooperate with each other, and that kind of thing. I think if we work toward peace as children, when we grow up we won't want to start a war, and we won't want to hurt each other. What we do as kids today for peace really matters just as much as what we do as adults tomorrow!

TOMORROW'S HERO

A famous artist once said that everyone on earth will have fifteen minutes of fame—fifteen minutes alone in the spotlight to say to the world, "This is who I am, and this is what I did."

For the most part, the kids in this book are ordinary kids, just like you. But at the same time, they are extraordinary kids—just like you. The only difference is that they have had their fifteen minutes.

If you're lucky, you'll never need to perform a rescue.

If you're lucky, you'll never have to prove your courage through your own hardships.

And nobody expects you to fly a plane before you drive a car, or find a cure for cancer before you graduate from high school . . .

. . . but still, somehow, you'll get that opportunity to be a hero in your own way—a chance to be someone that other people can look up to. And when that happens, you'll realize something remarkable.

You've been a hero all along.

Bibliography

Tony Aliengena

Associated Press. "Aviator, 11, Takes Off for Soviet and World Trip." *New York Times*, June 6, 1989.

Brodeur, Nicole. "Go Show the World How to Do It." *Orange County Register*, April 2, 1988.

Beene, Richard, and Jim Carlton, "Boy Propels Himself into the Record Book." *Los Angeles Times*, July 23, 1989, pp. 3, 34.

Carlton, Jim. "11-Year-Old O.C. Pilot Ready for Global Trip." *Los Angeles Times*, June 4, 1989, pp. 1, 3, 36.

_____. "Tony Lands in the Record Book." *Orange County Register*, April 3, 1988.

Neill, Michael. "A 9-Year-Old Californian Takes a Giant Step for Kidkind . . ." *People Weekly*, April 25, 1988, pp. 50–54.

James Bliemeister
Associated Press. "Boy Uses Head and Jaws to Save Day." *New York Newsday*, February 16, 1988.

Chrystal Booko
Borzi, Pat. "Water Skier Stands on Her Own 2 Feet." *Miami Herald*, January 8, 1988, p. 1PB.

"Lookout: A Guide to the Up and Coming." *People Weekly*, September 5, 1988, p. 65.

Juan Cordova
"A Fearless Fifth Grader." *Newsweek*, July 4, 1988, p. 48.

Tammy Crites
Rios, Denise A. "Loma Linda Children Survive Crash." *San Bernardino Sun*, August 16, 1986.

Ruth, Connie. "Girls Who Survive Crash Said Stable." *San Bernardino Sun*, August 17, 1986.

Wheeler, Carla. "Family Will Wait to Decide Future of Orphaned Sisters." *San Bernardino Sun*, August 25, 1986.

_____. "Mechanical Problems Ruled Out in Canadian Mountain Plane Crash." *San Bernardino Sun*, August 21, 1986.

Fatuma Dhidha
Associated Press. "Jousting with Jaws at River." *New York Newsday*, May 12, 1986.

Janet Evans
Anderson, Bruce. "Of Gold and Glee." *Sports Illustrated*, October 3, 1988, pp. 56–57.

Ewald, Russ. "Evans Goes the Distance." *Swimming World*, February 1988, pp. 26–32.

Lieber, Jill. "Meet a Small Wonder." *Sports Illustrated*, September 14, 1988, pp. 140–143.

Neff, Craig. "Her Golden Moment." *Sports Illustrated*, September 26, 1988, pp. 64–71.

Jason Gaes
Cohn, Victor. " 'If You Get Cansur, Don't Be Scared . . .' " *Washington Post*, April 26, 1988.

Gaes, Jason. *My Book for Kids with Cansur: A Child's Autobiography of Hope* (Aberdeen, South Dakota: Melius & Peterson Publishing, Inc., 1987).

"An Author with a Different Message," *Newsweek*, July 4, 1988, p. 41.

"Jason's Happy Ending," *Reader's Digest*, July 1988, p. 152.

Felipe Garza
Hughes, Polly Ross. "Girl Learns She Received Friend's Heart." *San Francisco Chronicle*, January 8, 1986, p. 1.

_____. "The Short, Hard Life of Boy Who Willed His Heart." *San Francisco Chronicle*, January 17, 1986, p. 3.

John and Tony Gomez
DePaola, Gina. "After Parents Leave, Brothers Make It on Own." *San Bernardino Sun*, June 19, 1988.

_____. "Readers Pour in Donations to S.B. Twins." *San Bernardino Sun*, June 24, 1988.

Scott and Matthew Higa
"Double Trouble." *Kid City News*, June 19, 1989, p. 21.

Mewhinney, Mike. "Tiny Twins Have Moxie to Spare." *San Francisco Progress*, May 18, 1986, pp. 1–2.

Pham Hong
"21 Heroes Under 21," *McCalls*, July 1986, p. 49.

Patrick Hood, Raymond Smith, Michael Wissman
Schwartz, Addam. "Ryan Students Overpower Their Captor." *Northeast Times*, January 14, 1986.

Milla Jovovich
"Lookout: A Guide to the Up and Coming." *People Weekly*, June 6, 1988, p. 151.

Sean Kingsley
Associated Press. "Boy, 5, Holds on to Save Cousin's Life." *Medford Mail Tribune*, February 16, 1988.

Amanda Lawrence
Neergaard, Lauran. "7-Year-Old 'Coach' Helps with Birth." *Valley Times News* (Atlanta), May 17, 1989, p. 1.

United Press International. "Girl, 7, Calmly Helps Mom Deliver Baby." *Rockdale Citizen*, May 17, 1989.

"Lake City Youngster Helps Mother in Labor." *Kennesaw Neighbor*, May 18, 1989, p. 1.

Brent Meldrum
Associated Press. "Whatever You Call It, It Saved His Pal's Life." *New York Newsday*, August 6, 1986.

Zebulon Roche
"Lookout: A Guide to the Up and Coming." *People Weekly*, April 11, 1988, pp. 79–80.

Scout Troup 223
Kahler, Karl. "Devoted Leader Inspires Scouts to Soar as Eagles." *Los Angeles Times*, January 8, 1989, Westside Section, pp. 1, 8.

Ignat Solzhenitsyn
Neuhaus, Cable. "Kin." *People Weekly*, July 20, 1987, p. 91.

Sage Volkman
Klein, Julie. "A Courage Beyond Understanding." *People Weekly*, March 21, 1988, pp. 28–32.

"A Family Rises Above Pain." *Newsweek*, July 4, 1988, p. 49.

Ryan White
Friedman, Jack, and Bill Shaw. "The Quiet Victories of Ryan White." *People Weekly*, May 30, 1988, pp. 88–96.

Servaas, Cory, M.D. "The Happier Days for Ryan White." *Saturday Evening Post*, March 1988, pp. 88–96.

Tian Ying
"Lookout: A Guide to the Up and Coming." *People Weekly*, May 2, 1988, p. 117.

Other Sources

The Carnegie Hero Fund Commission provided information on the following:

> Gregory Dickens, Leatrice Harrison, Joseph Jackson, Lawrence Weigand III, and all the "Kids to Remember."

Hasbro's G.I. Joe Search for Real American Heroes provided information on the following:

> Colleen Cooke, Shane Dodd, Michelle Lampert, John Lynch, Chrissie McKenney, Freddie Self, Hector Sierra, and Angela Thornton.

Optimist International provided information on the following:

> Patrick Hood, Katrin Hubenthal, Raymond Smith, and Michael Wissman.

Young American Magazine provided information on the following:

> Michelle Alexander, Terry Butler, Betsy Clarke, Janet Evans, Felipe Garza, Damon Kheir-Eldin,

Chris LaFortuna, Jamar Mitchell, Denise Parker, David Peterson, Sam "Ricky Rocko" Rogoway, Robert Scruton, Dalit Paz Warshaw, and Segura Williams.

Information on the following were taken from actual interviews:

Michelle Alexander, Tony Aliengena, Ray Bateman, Jr., Colleen Cooke, Sacajuwea Hunter, Joseph Jackson, Rocky Lyons, Chrissie McKenney, Joe Memory, Laurinda Mulhaupt, Sharla Ramsey, Sam "Ricky Rocko" Rogoway, and Jeff Wood.

Would You Like to Write to Any of the Kid Heroes in This Book?

Address your letters to:

Kid Heroes
c/o Neal Shusterman
RGA Publishing Group
1875 Century Park East, Suite 220
Los Angeles, CA 90067